"I don't regret sp
but I'm afraid I've caused a problem between
us."

"I can deal with it if you can." Oksana's crazy heart started going nuts. He was so close. And so beautiful.

"But if I hadn't brought the chair today, we wouldn't have anything to deal with."

"That's where you're wrong." She dredged up a smile. "We just wouldn't have acknowledged it. Now we have. Maybe that's better."

"If you say so."

"We don't ever have to speak of it again, though."

He nodded. "Understood."

"But..." Did she dare? Oh, hell, it was now or never. "Since this is it, and we're putting everything behind us, would you... kiss me before you go?"

WRANGLING THE COWBOY'S DREAMS

ROWDY RANCH

Vicki Lewis Thompson

Ocean Dance Press

WRANGLING THE COWBOY'S DREAMS
© 2024 Vicki Lewis Thompson

ISBN: 978-1-63803-925-9

Ocean Dance Press LLC
PO Box 69901
Oro Valley, AZ 85737

Visit the author's website at
VickiLewisThompson.com

Want more cowboys? Check out these other titles by Vicki Lewis Thompson

Rowdy Ranch

Having the Cowboy's Baby
Stoking the Cowboy's Fire
Testing the Cowboy's Resolve
Rocking the Cowboy's Christmas
Roping the Cowboy's Heart
Tempting the Cowboy's Sister
Craving the Cowboy's Kiss
Heating Up the Cowboy's Christmas
Wrangling the Cowboy's Dreams

The Buckskin Brotherhood

Sweet-Talking Cowboy
Big-Hearted Cowboy
Baby-Daddy Cowboy
True-Blue Cowboy
Strong-Willed Cowboy
Secret-Santa Cowboy
Stand-Up Cowboy
Single-Dad Cowboy
Marriage-Minded Cowboy
Gift-Giving Cowboy

The McGavin Brothers

A Cowboy's Strength
A Cowboy's Honor
A Cowboy's Return
A Cowboy's Heart
A Cowboy's Courage
A Cowboy's Christmas
A Cowboy's Kiss

<u>*1*</u>

Traffic was light on the 93 coming home from Missoula Saturday morning. That suited Lucky McLintock just fine. He and his two companions would be back in Wagon Train before the snow hit. He needed to get that red chair unloaded from the bed of his pickup, too.

"Good thing we got this done when we did." His brother Rance was wedged in the back seat next to a garment bag of rented wedding duds. "Those big ol' clouds over the Sapphires are on the move."

Trenton Armstrong, better known as Trent, occupied the front passenger seat. "I appreciate you two devoting your Saturday morning to picking up the clothes." He'd relocated to Montana just in time to be best man at his brother Dallas's wedding.

"Happy to help." Lucky flashed him a smile. Trent had been all set to go it alone, since Dallas was banking time at the fire station to give him extra days for a honeymoon. "Gave me an excuse to check out the furniture store sale." And surprise Oksana.

"That chair's a beauty," said Rance, who'd invited himself along for the ride. "Killer price, too, and they threw in the ottoman for practically nothing. Oksana will love it."

"Have I met this lady?" Trent's brow furrowed. "I've been trying to place her."

"She's my assistant at the bookstore."

"Oh! I was thinking girlfriend."

Lucky smiled. "No, not at all."

"Must be a valued employee, then. You were very particular about the color and whether it would fit her right."

"She's valued, all right, and I happen to know red's her favorite color. Also, she's tall, at least five-ten, so—"

"Five-ten? Did you say five-ten?" Rance leaned forward, mimicking the salesman's voice. "Gosh almighty, folks, this is your lucky day because I'm five-ten on the button. Let's just have us a de-mon-stra-tion."

Lucky snorted. "When he let out a big ol' sigh and closed his eyes, I figured I'd better grab it for Oksana before he bought it for himself."

"Unusual first name," Trent said. "I've heard it somewhere, but I can't remember—"

"She's named after Oksana Baiul, the figure skater." Which had been a mixed blessing for her.

"Right. That's where I've heard it. So why are you buying her an easy chair? Is she elderly? Does she have a health issue?"

"She's twenty-seven and in great shape— I mean *health*. She's in great health." As her employer, he had no business thinking about her shape.

Trent still looked confused. "Is it for the bookstore? Because I can see customers wanting to—"

"It isn't. We already have a couple of chairs in a reading nook. No ottomans. We don't want customers taking a nap. This'll go in her apartment above the store."

"Ah. Good idea. Everyone needs a comfy chair."

"I agree, and the one she has is uncomfortable, especially for reading. I know because that's where I lived when I first took over managing the store."

"I get it. She mentioned the chair and now you're replacing it. That's a thoughtful move."

"She's never mentioned the chair. She wouldn't. She's a fanatic about watching the bottom line. I've been thinking about this for a while, and finally decided I had to buy it instead of putting it on the store's credit card."

"Wow. She sounds like the perfect employee. "What's her last name?"

"Jones."

"Oksana Jones. I like that. An unusual first name paired with one of the most common last names in the country. Is she coming to the wedding?"

"She is."

"Good. Then I'll get to meet her."

They'd probably like each other. Why did that give him a twinge?

Rance jumped in. "Oksana is *amazing*, dude. You can go in there and ask her about a book, any book, and she either hands it to you in under a minute or finds it online almost as fast. She barely needs Lucky around at all. Which reminds me, bro, she's due for a raise."

"I gave her one six months ago."

"Give her another one."

"She wouldn't accept it unless we'd had another uptick in sales, which we haven't. Christmas didn't count. It's seasonal." He put on his signal and passed an SUV that was lollygagging. Clearly the driver didn't have the same respect for those bulging clouds that he did.

"Okay, then take her to dinner."

"Uh... no, I don't think that would be—"

"Make it a *business* dinner if you must. You can sit there and go over your spreadsheets, but at least you could treat her to a nice meal. It doesn't have to be a date. Then again, I can't remember the last time you asked somebody out. You've probably forgotten how."

"The store's been busy. The holidays, the Santa display at the fair, then inventory, then—"

"That dog won't hunt, bro. Ever since you hired her that place has been running like my supercharged V-8. You could take the time and she deserves a reward. Treat her to dinner at the Buffalo."

"Hey, I bought her a chair." But his brother was right. Oksana had earned a dinner at the Buffalo. Several dinners.

But he was hesitant. He and Oksana enjoyed a sweet tension that was harmless at its current level. He didn't want to mess with that, and not just because of the employer/employee relationship.

He used to date, even got serious about someone a couple years ago, but when she'd started pushing for a ring, he'd backed off. He turned twenty-eight this year. Most women in his age group were looking for a commitment. But he was firmly on the fence in that department.

"Good thing you moved here, Trent," Rance continued. "It'll be great to have another bachelor around who's putting himself out there. We can trade war stories. I'll bet you're not letting grass grow under your feet."

"You'd lose that bet," Trent said. "I have enough grass under my feet to keep the ranch horses fed for a month."

"That can't be right. I've seen you on the dance floor at the Buffalo. Are you telling me you haven't asked any of those women for their digits?"

"That's what I'm telling you. I've had my hands full learning to dance country style. One thing at a time."

Rance pursued the subject. "Ever heard of multitasking? You're a decent looking guy and being Dallas's brother gives ladies a point of reference."

"Yeah, but I'm not a firefighter. Or a cowboy. I'm a product manager."

"Well, I wouldn't lead with that list of negatives, but—"

"What product do you manage?" Lucky's ears perked up. This was the first concrete detail he'd heard about Trent's job. He'd mentioned he could live anywhere with good Wi-Fi, which had allowed him to rent Cheyenne's cabin and give

Montana a try. But he hadn't divulged any particulars.

"Depends on the client. Businesses hire me when they're developing a new product or service. I research the market and help them create a launch plan."

"So, let's say L'Amour and More wanted to open a second bookstore in a nearby town. You could help with that?"

"Absolutely. Are you thinking about it?"

"Not any time soon. Just curious. What are you working on, now?"

"A company hired me to research the novelty condom market."

Rance cracked up. "Sure they did."

"God's truth. The research data's on my laptop, but since it's proprietary, I can't show it to you."

"I'll bet Rance can give you some data." Lucky deadpanned the delivery. "Hey, bro, was it just candy canes and wreaths on those, or was there a Santa—"

"Never mind." Rance's scowl appeared in the rearview mirror. Then he switched his attention to Trent. "Does this company also make the regular kind?"

"They do."

"Then you should tell them to scrub the project. Guys want their lady hot and bothered, not giggling so hard she can't breathe."

"Good info." Trent's cough sounded like stifled laughter. "The company's looking at sales, but they might not be considering customer satisfaction."

"Well, this customer was extremely *dis*satisfied. And I wouldn't recommend describing your current project to a lady friend."

"Wasn't planning to."

"Matter of fact, I wouldn't mention your job at all. Concentrate on your look. The clothes Dallas talked you into are a big improvement. You might consider trading in that sedan for a truck, though."

"I don't need one."

"It's part of your look. If you dress like a cowboy and drive a truck, you can let women assume—"

"That I'm a cowpoke from Jersey? The minute I open my mouth, they'll know I'm not the real deal."

"Then don't talk much. Be mysterious."

"I think you're smart to take it slow," Lucky stepped in before Rance dispensed any more of his harebrained advice. "Give yourself time to get acclimated. Dallas sounded just like you when he first got here, but now he has a slight drawl and tosses out *yes, ma'ams* like he was born to it."

"I noticed he's gone country. My sisters are gonna tease the living daylights out of him, which will take their minds off the prospect of being eaten alive by wolves and grizzlies."

Lucky rolled his eyes. "C'mon. They don't really think—"

"I'm exaggerating, but they're kinda ramped up about it. My parents, too. They've never been out West. Logically they know bears hibernate in the winter, but that still leaves wolves and mountain lions. They're not wrong about the wolves. I've heard them howling."

Lucky turned onto the dirt road to Rowdy Ranch. "It's not like they'll break into your house and eat you up like in the storybooks."

"Intellectually, they know that." He shrugged. "Unknowns can be scary, though, especially if you have a vivid imagination."

"I take it they're a lot younger than you." Rance sounded disappointed by that prospect.

"Not much. Atlanta's twenty-eight and Syracuse is twenty-six."

"Oh!" That perked up his brother considerably. "Do they go by those names?"

"They use Lani and Sara."

"Much better. Not that naming kids after where they were conceived isn't way cool, but—"

"Lani doesn't think so. She keeps threatening to change hers. Sara thinks it's funny. Anyway, they've scared themselves by watching too many wildlife specials, but they'll be fine once they get here."

"Just leave them to me." Rance's enthusiasm returned. "You and Dallas will be busy with the wedding and Lucky keeps saying he's consumed by work. I'll put myself in charge of watching out for your folks."

Lucky grinned. "You do that, bro." Rance would keep a close eye on those sisters, all right. When it came to women, his spirit of adventure never flagged.

He dropped Trent and the stuffed garment bag off at Cheyenne's cabin. Everyone still referred to it as Cheyenne's even though his older brother hadn't lived there for a couple of years. Would Trent finally be the one to buy it? Too soon to tell.

Rance climbed into the front seat for the short trip to his place. "I like that guy. I think we need to get him on a horse, though. And take him shopping for an F-150."

"What if he'd rather have a Ram?"

"We'll talk him out of it. If he's living on McLintock property, he needs a Ford. It's what we drive." He peered out the windshield. "Looks like it'll snow any minute."

"That's why I'm just gonna drop you off quick and head on back to town."

"Are you sure about that? We could take the chair to your place and haul it inside. She's been without a good one for months. A couple of nights doesn't matter."

"You're right, but now that I have it, I want to take it to her."

"It'll probably get snowed on."

"The tarp will protect it."

"You'll likely be unloading it while it's snowing. You should have let him wrap it in plastic."

"Makes it harder to grip."

Rance sighed. "Have it your way. Turn around. I'm going with you."

"No, you're not. This is your day off. You love having a day off. You never shut up about the glory of a whole day off and you've already lost half of it." He pulled up next to Rance's cabin. "Go on. Get out of here."

"What if you get stuck in town?"

"I have options. I have a key to McLintock Metalworks and there's a bed in the back room. And Mrs. J's told me several times she'll find a spot at her B&B if I need a place to crash."

"Alrighty, then. Once you get that steely look on your face, there's no budging you. Just text me and let me know where you end up."

"I will. And thanks for the help today."

"It was solely for my benefit. My jacket for Marsh and Ella's wedding was a lousy fit. Threw me off my game. And with Trent's sisters in the mix this time, I plan to be on my game."

"They could have fiancés or steady boyfriends back home."

"Maybe, but I think Trent would've said so." He opened his door. "Don't forget. Text me."

"I promise."

Rance flashed him a thumbs up, swung down and closed the door.

Tapping the horn in farewell, Lucky backed the truck around and headed toward the ranch road. The role reversal with his brother made him smile. Normally he was the one making Rance check in.

Although they'd arrived in the world only two hours apart, they were nothing alike. Rance was impetuous and outgoing, while he was cautious and reserved. That made sense, in a way.

Rance had been born a McLintock, his background an open book. Lucky's origins remained shrouded in mystery. He'd inherited his Irish mother's green eyes and dark hair. Beyond that he was a blank slate.

But Desiree McLintock had swooped in and added him to her brood. He gave thanks for that miracle every single day.

<u>2</u>

Snow flurries whirled outside the multi-paned bay window of L'Amour and More. Oksana gazed past the display of books, a few shiny red hearts and three adorable Cupids dangling from red ribbons.

The street was empty, not a person or vehicle in sight. She should give up, flip the sign over and make herself a toasted cheese sandwich. Mother Nature had given her the afternoon off.

But first she wanted to hear from Lucky. By now he should be safely tucked into his cabin at Rowdy Ranch. But since she hadn't heard from him, he must still be on the road.

Crossing to the cash wrap, she picked up her phone to check whether she'd missed a text. Nope. Then she opened her map app to look for traffic issues on the 93. Didn't find any. Huh.

He was scheduled to work this afternoon but he wasn't a stupid man. He'd cancel that plan for a snowstorm. He'd also text her to let her know. Always had before.

Taking down her ponytail, she finger-combed her hair and replaced the red scrunchie — a nervous habit when she was on edge. If something had happened, no one would think to call her, not for a long time, anyway.

Damn it, why hadn't he—

The rumble of a truck engine sent her running to the window. What the heck was he doing here? He knew as well as anyone they'd have zero customers during a snowstorm and no task in the store merited driving to town during bad weather. What could he possibly—

"Hey." He hurried in with a grin on his handsome face, his cheeks flushed from the cold and his neatly-trimmed beard decorated with melting flakes. "Wait'll you see what I found."

"Did you happen to notice it's snow—"

"Stand by the door so you can open it when I come back."

"Are you going to tell me what this is about?"

"I'd rather show you." Shoving his keys in his pocket, he ducked out the door and pulled on a pair of gloves as he headed for the back of his truck.

The diagonal parking space allowed her a partial view of a large object covered with a tarp. Once he started wrestling it free, the color emerged. Fire-engine red. Tilting it sideways, he hugged it to his chest and started toward her.

A chair. She was so stunned she almost forgot to open the door. Pulling it wide, she shivered as freezing air billowed in. "Can I do something?"

"I've got it." Panting, he maneuvered the upholstered chair through the opening, his gloves brushing the door jam.

Once he was clear, she closed the door, teeth chattering. "For the s-store?"

"For you." He set it down with a thump. "For upstairs."

"What?"

He gulped for air. "You need a new one."

"We can't afford—"

"I can, and although you haven't complained, I know that old chair is the worst. I've been thinking about this for more than a year and I finally couldn't stand it anymore, picturing you hunched in that lousy excuse for a reading chair."

Her jaw dropped. He'd bought her an easy chair. With his money. How could she accept it?

"Don't look like that. It was on sale. There's a matching ottoman. I'll be right back."

She stared after him as he dashed out again. Then her attention returned to the chair. She touched the soft fabric. Caressed it. Although she didn't believe in love at first sight, this chair could change her thinking on the subject.

When he fumbled with the door, she snapped out of her daze long enough to grab the knob and tug it open. "Sorry!"

"No worries. I almost had it. This isn't heavy, mostly because it's hollow. You can store stuff in it." He placed the ottoman in front of the chair. "Try it out. I want to see if it fits you."

"Are you kidding? Of course it will fit me, but I can't believe you bought it. I was fine with the other one."

"Liar."

"I'm a tenant in a furnished apartment. The furniture is supposed to be utilitarian, not luxurious."

"Except when it comes to an easy chair when the tenant happens to be a voracious reader. The floor lamp is okay, but that sorry excuse for a— anyway, never mind." He pulled off his gloves and tucked them in his jacket pocket. "Just sit in it, please. I need to know if it'll work out before we haul it up there."

"Okay, but I'm paying you back for it."

"No, you're not."

"I am." She nudged the ottoman out of the way and sank down. The chair embraced her like a lover — warm and firm, yet supple and giving.

He chuckled. "That's the sigh I was listening for."

"I sighed?" She met his green gaze. His eyes sparkled with so much joy that she instantly regretted her initial reaction to his generous gift. "Okay, I love it." She took a deep breath. "And I handled your incredible gesture poorly. I'm so sorry. Thank you for this gorgeous chair."

"You're welcome. Put your feet up and see how that feels."

"Not with my boots on." Leaning over, she yanked them off.

"The material's supposed to be forgiving. You don't have to baby it."

"But I will." She rested her feet on the ottoman and leaned back. This time she sighed on purpose. "Heaven." She looked up at him. "And it's red."

"I've been on the lookout for a red one for months." He unbuttoned his coat. "Then this week the stars aligned so I volunteered to help Trent pick up the groomsmen outfits from the rental place."

She bolted upright. "And now you need to get in your truck immediately and drive back to the ranch before the snow gets any worse."

"Not until we haul this upstairs. You're mighty, but it'll take two people to accomplish that."

"We can leave it here for the weekend."

"No, ma'am. I set out to do this and I refuse to leave it partially completed. Not my style."

"Then let's get to it." She put on her boots and stood. "I'll take the top and back up the stairs if you'll take the bottom."

"That's the way I had it figured. Is your door open?"

"Can't remember. I'll go check." She walked quickly to the back of the store and scampered up the stairs. Had she tidied up this morning? If not, too bad. She couldn't take time now. Halfway up she could see that she'd left her door open, so she turned around and headed back down. "Door's— oh, you're here already. Good."

He'd ditched his hat, leaving an adorable crease in his curly dark hair. "We probably need to turn it sideways, like I did to get it into the shop."

"My thought, too." She moved up next to the chair, laid one hand on the back and the other on the arm. "Whenever you're ready."

"On three." He crouched by the base and got a grip on the chair. "One, two, *three.*"

She took the weight of the top half as he rolled it to one side.

He held her gaze. "Don't rush. I'll synchronize my moves to yours."

"Got it." Glancing over her shoulder, she backed toward the bottom step. "I'm glad the stairs don't have a bend."

"Or a spiral. Some two-stories downtown have that. I used to wish this one did until the day the refrigerator conked out."

"At least this is lighter than a refrigerator." She tightened her grip. "Let's do it." Backing up one step, she felt the weight shift toward Lucky. "You okay?"

"I've got it."

She backed up another step, then one more.

Lucky stayed with her, his breathing growing harsher as they ascended.

"Need a break?"

"Keep going. I knew it was heavy. That's what I wanted."

"I'm at the landing. Gotta make a slight turn to the right."

"Should work." Sweat made his dark curls stick to his forehead.

Her muscles strained a little, too, but he had the tough part. She eased the chair past the railing and through the open door. "Almost there."

"I'm right with you."

"Once you're in, let's just put it down. I can take it from here."

"Nah, I wanna see how it looks with the ottoman." He lowered the base to the wooden floor. "Hang on. I'll be right back."

"But I can carry—" Too late. He was gone, clattering down the stairs. "You need to get going!" she called after him."

"I will."

"Would you please turn off the shop lights while you're down there?"

"Yes, ma'am!"

She took a quick survey of the rectangular apartment — bedroom and bath to her right, sitting area in front of her, kitchen and laundry closet to her left. The bed was made, the dishes washed and sitting in the strainer, *and red undies were air-drying on her stainless-steel laundry rack.*

Hot-footing it to the rack, she managed to snatch up one bra before he reappeared carrying the ottoman. Rather than standing there holding a bra, she dropped it back in place. "You're fast."

"Had to be. Somebody keeps trying to shove me out the door."

"Because I don't want you getting stuck on the way home."

"You can rest your mind about that." He set the ottoman in front of the chair.

"It's let up?"

"No, ma'am. We've got us a full-fledged blizzard out there. Only a fool would attempt to drive any distance in that."

"Now that you mention it, I can hear the wind." He couldn't leave? Were they snowed in together? Her heart thumped a little faster. "So… what will you do?"

He smiled. "I'm not going to crash with you, if that's what's put that look of panic on your face."

"But this is your shop." She took a deep breath and willed herself to calm down. "You're welcome to stay here."

"Don't worry, that wasn't my plan. Mrs. J said she'd find space at the B&B if I ever needed it."

"Oh. Then you'd better call her. And drive over there before it gets any worse."

"When you're right, you're right." He pulled his phone out of his pocket. "I had the same thought when I looked outside, or rather *tried* to look outside. You can't see the lamppost in front of the store, let alone the street."

"Wow. Can you even make it to the B&B?"

"Probably can if my GPS talks me through it."

"At least nobody should be on the road." She walked over to the only window upstairs, which was over the kitchen sink. The second story apartment had been an afterthought, perched on the back half of the building's roof. Obviously windows hadn't been a priority.

Parting the curtains, she stared at a wall of white as snow pelted the window. Soon it would be iced over.

Behind her, Lucky talked with Mrs. J, who'd recently opened Wagon Train's first B&B with her granddaughter Molly. When Bret and Molly had tied the knot last year, Mrs. J had become family.

"No, really, Mrs. J. I'll be perfectly fine in Bret and Gil's shop. It's cozy. And only a block away.

I'm all set. Yes, ma'am, I'll call if for some reason it doesn't work out, but I'm sure it will. Stay warm, now. 'Bye."

She turned toward him. "She's booked?"

"Up to her ears. I should have realized she would be. With Valentine's Day on Wednesday, she's running a couples' special this weekend and next. Folks gobbled it up." He shrugged. "No worries. Bret and Gil have all the necessities in the back of their shop — bed, bathroom, fridge and stove."

"What about food?"

"There's probably something."

"You don't sound very sure about that. You should eat before you go."

He frowned. "I don't want to impose on—"

"No imposition at all. I was about to have a toasted cheese sandwich. Want to join me?"

He brightened. "I'll admit that sounds terrific. Will you let me help?"

"Depends. Are you handy in the kitchen?"

"Yes, ma'am. We all are. Mom wouldn't have it any other way. She was determined to turn out fully functioning adults."

"Then let's make some lunch." The prospect generated a buzz, a sensual one. She'd never shared a meal with her boss. Now they'd be cooking one together.

On top of it, he'd bought her a chair. Was the dynamic shifting? Did she want it to?

3

"First I need to text Rance." Lucky typed a quick message. "I promised him I'd let him know my situation. He tried to talk me out of driving in."

"I thought he was the wild and crazy one."

"He is, but lately he's mellowing, becoming a lot more considerate of others and not so focused on himself." When his brother texted back a thumbs-up emoji, he tucked his phone away. "But he's still Rance. He'll likely be the life of the party at the wedding reception next week."

"I had so much fun at Marsh and Ella's wedding last year. I can't wait for this one. Angie was sweet to invite me."

"She's been a fan of yours ever since she found out you've read every single book M.R. Morrison has written, even the Ranch Puppy series." He kept talking while he pretended to ignore the red undies she was quietly removing from the metal drying rack.

"Why wouldn't I? He's a terrific writer."

"No argument there." Since everything on the rack was red, then logically that's what she had on now — an image he'd ditch immediately.

"If he knew how much he's loved in Wagon Train and how we faithfully promote him in L'Amour and More, I think he'd make an exception to his *no public appearances* rule and do a signing here."

Cheeks flushed, she shoved her red bras and panties in the dresser over near the bed without bothering to fold anything. She closed the drawer and faced him. "I keep writing his publisher, but so far, nada."

He grabbed onto the conversational thread with relief. "You're writing to them? I didn't know that."

"I was hoping to surprise you with a confirmation, but going through the publisher isn't working." She walked back over to the kitchen and pulled a frying pan out of the cupboard. "I just get a form letter saying that M.R. Morrison doesn't make public appearances."

"That's what I've heard, too." She'd get nowhere with his mom's publisher because they were convinced keeping the secret was the way to go. "Got a job for me?"

"You can take the cheese out of the fridge. And some apple cider. I thought we'd warm it up, unless you—"

"Warm cider suits me fine."

She took an unsliced loaf from the bread box and a cutting board from a hook on the wall. "I'll handle the bread if you'll slice the cheese. There's another cutting board under the — oh, why am I telling you?" She laughed. "I keep forgetting you lived here."

"It's been a few years, but I remember that much." He reached under the lip of the counter and slid out the built-in cutting board. When his mom had bought this building twenty years ago, the workmanship on the upstairs cabinets had been a selling point.

The irregularly shaped block of cheddar cheese was his favorite brand. He had to get creative with the slicing so he had the right configuration to cover the surface of the bread.

Oksana turned on the heat under the skillet. "I suppose he could be infirm or have a phobia of some kind."

"Who?"

"M.R. Morrison."

"Oh." He hid a smile. His mom was the opposite of infirm or phobic. "Or just very private. Not everybody likes the spotlight."

"I understand, but I think he'd feel right at home in this adorable little bookshop. Assuming he doesn't have a serious mental or physical health issue, he could bask in the love of his readers for an afternoon. Would that be so terrible?"

"Doesn't sound so bad when you put it that way." He'd never considered the possibility that his mom was missing out on one of the perks of her chosen career.

Buttered bread sizzled in the pan. "I'm ready for the cheese."

He pulled the board all the way out and handed it over.

"Nice job. You're hired."

He laughed. "If you think that's great, you should see me open the cider and pour it into a pan. Those are skills you don't come across every day."

"Smartass." She flashed him a grin. Then her eyes widened. "Whoops. I just called my boss a smartass."

"Call it like you see it, lady." Those big brown eyes were so expressive. He plain liked her. A lot. Good thing this interlude had an end point. Too much togetherness could lead to places neither of them needed to go.

Moments later they sat across from each other at her bistro-sized kitchen table. She'd positioned the table so it had a view of the sitting area and its small cast-iron heater that mimicked the flicker of a wood stove.

The cozy apartment could accommodate two people, just barely. They'd avoided collisions so far, but one was inevitable when there was only so much room and he'd just added another big piece of furniture.

She'd busted out some chips to go with the sandwich and he helped himself to a handful. "Thanks for feeding me."

"You're welcome, but I'll bet one sandwich won't be enough."

"Yes, it will."

"Tell the truth, now. You don't maintain what I'd guesstimate is around two-twenty by eating one cheese sandwich and a few chips for lunch. You're just hesitant about using up my stash."

"You weren't exactly expecting me."

"No, but I read the weather report yesterday and stocked up at the market. That's why I bought that big hunk of cheese." She took a bite.

"Which I'm happy about. This brand of cheddar makes a great cheese sandwich." He tucked in and hummed with pleasure.

"I also have a spare loaf of bread, so I insist you have another sandwich. I would have made three but the frying pan only holds two."

He chewed and swallowed. "Will you have a second one?"

"I will. As you can tell, I'm not a delicate flower. I can eat."

"So can I. Especially in winter, when I need to split firewood several times a week." Maybe it was the sandwich and maybe it was the company, but he was totally enjoying the meal.

"Splitting firewood sounds more exciting than running, which is my exercise of choice. Or rather, the only one available to me these days."

"You played sports, right?"

"Basketball, mostly. I was on the JV team of my tiny school during the state tournament when Ella was Wagon Train's star. I idolized her."

"Does she know that?"

"I made a point of telling her the first time she came into the shop. Since then we've squeezed in a few coffee dates so we can talk b-ball."

Mouth full, he nodded in approval.

"Even better, over this past Christmas break she invited me down to the gym a couple of times for a game of horse. We had a blast."

"Ella's terrific. I'm glad Marsh finally got smart." He wasn't surprised that Oksana had made friends since she'd moved to town. She made them easily, more easily than he did. "Have you ever wanted to be a coach?"

"Thought about it, but counseling is my first love. I want to be there for the kids who are different, like me. I had to deal with my size. And my name. My poor mom. She meant well."

"It's distinctive." Picking up his mug, he savored a mouthful of warm, tangy cider.

"When you're five feet tall and eight years old that's the last thing you want. But a counselor helped me get through it and I want to do the same for the ones who're made to feel self-conscious about something they can't help."

"You'll be great at it. I hate the idea of losing you, but—"

"You won't for a while. I'm hoping the fall semester will be my last, but it depends on what I'm able to register for."

"I don't know how that works. I've considered taking a marketing class but I know zip about the online routine."

"It's pretty easy. I'll show you." She got up and fetched her laptop. While they ate their second sandwich, she explained the process for registering and submitting assignments.

"Very helpful. Thanks." He finished off his cider and put down his mug. "And thanks for a delicious lunch. Let's clean up the dishes and then I'll head over to Bret and Gil's shop."

"Don't feel like you have to go immediately. I doubt there's much to do down there and we both have some time off courtesy of the blizzard."

"True, but I'll bet normally you'd use it to catch up on your classes."

"I might, or I might decide to goof off and study tonight. Want to goof off with me?"

She was inviting him to stay for a while longer. Lord knows he wanted to. Driving through a blizzard to arrive at Bret and Gil's unoccupied shop and hang out there by himself was as appealing as digging a post hole in the rain.

"I can tell you're not eager to head out. And I'll bet you play chess."

"I do."

"Are you any good?"

He smiled. "Are you?"

"Only one way for you to find out."

He gazed at her, so tempted to relax into the moment and so conflicted about making that decision.

"C'mon, Lucky. We have the perfect setup — two easy chairs with the ottoman in the middle for the board. We can position ourselves next to the little fake wood stove and have another mug of warm cider. Doesn't that sound like fun?"

"Yes, ma'am." He threw caution to the winds. "It surely does."

4

Coaxing Lucky to stick around was risky. Oksana liked her job, her boss and her boss's boss, Desiree McLintock.

The apartment over the shop was cozy and put her steps away from work. Since she lived in the heart of town, she rarely had to drive anywhere. That saved her time and money, and she needed both to continue her education.

If her situation couldn't be any better, was she taking a chance on making it worse by hosting her boss for the afternoon and possibly the evening? He was attracted to her, although he was fighting it. She appreciated that because she had a crush on him, too.

Acting on that crush wasn't smart. A physical attraction to a handsome man had tripped her up before and she wouldn't let it happen again. But how could she let the poor guy drive through a blizzard to a lonely backroom which might not be stocked with food?

"Thanks again for that tasty lunch." Lucky dried his plate and put it back in the cupboard.

"You're welcome. Just so you know, I made a big pot of stew last night. You can either eat it here or take it with you, but I'm gonna force it on you. The Metalworks shop is a place of business. I'd be shocked if you found the makings of a meal down there." She rinsed the frying pan and handed it to him.

"I doubt I would either, so I accept the offer, but I'll take it to go. A chess game sounds more exciting than sitting alone in the Metalworks shop with only a book for company, but I won't monopolize your evening, too." He finished drying the pan. "I don't know where you keep—"

"Under here." She opened a bottom cupboard door. "This is where the pots and pans were when I moved in. And thanks for providing them. I left mine in storage after I saw these. I've never had a matching set."

"Glad you like them. Remember me asking you if you planned to cook here?"

"Yes, and it seemed strange since the place has a kitchen. Of course I'd cook. It's cheaper than eating out."

"My mom wanted me to ask. Our last employee rarely cooked and when he did, he burned things. Nice guy, excellent at customer service, but the pots and pans got abused. No amount of scrubbing would save them, so she bought all new before you moved in."

"No wonder they're so shiny. But how did she know I wouldn't abuse the cookware?"

"She didn't, but I told her you were a safe bet."

"How could *you* know that?"

"Your old truck is clean inside and out. It also runs well. That's why I asked you to—"

"Give you a ride to the Buffalo? That threw me. It's not that far."

"Far enough that I can check out how you care for your vehicle. I do that with every prospective employee since they'll be living upstairs."

"Then how did the pan scorcher slip through?"

"His vehicle was reasonably clean but it ran rough. He said he was planning to take it in for a tune-up the following day, so I hired him. I doubt he ever had that tune-up."

"You know what I thought when you asked for a ride to the Buffalo?"

"That I was either lazy or late?"

"I couldn't picture you being either. But I've always heard that real cowboys hate walking anywhere, so evidently you purely despised it."

He grinned. "Then you must have been very confused when you took the job and saw me strolling all over town."

"I was dying to ask you about it but I couldn't figure out how, so I came up with my own explanation."

"I can't wait to hear it."

"I decided you'd gone in for a checkup and the doctor said you'd better walk a mile or two a day or you'd grow old and creaky before your time."

That cracked him up. She'd never seen him laugh that hard. He had to take a bandanna from his back pocket and wipe away the tears. "That's a riot. I have to tell Rance next time I see him. He'll love it." He folded the bandanna and tucked it back in his pocket. "The point is, I was right about you."

"As you've probably guessed, my family's not well off. Never has been. My parents dropped out when they were juniors in high school. That's when they had my brother. I came along four years later."

"Having kids when you're young can make it tough."

"Sure can. They told me and my brother to get an education and do it before we brought kids into the mix. He didn't listen, but I did."

"Are you sure you don't need to study? 'Cause I can take a container of stew and head down—"

"No, doggone it! I'm looking forward to this chess game. I'll probably be rusty since I haven't played since I started working here."

"Then we're even because it's been about the same for me. Rance and I used to play on his nights off, but he hasn't suggested it in... wow, I think our last game was at least a year ago."

"So it's settled. You're staying."

He chuckled. "Looks like it."

"Great. Go ahead and arrange the chairs. I'll get the chess set. I almost left it in storage, too, since I knew I'd be busy. Glad I didn't." Opening a bifold closet door, she pulled the large box down from the top shelf and carried it over to the ottoman.

"That looks substantial."

"Because it is. I got it in Spain."

"Spain? When were you in Spain?"

"That's a long story."

"I've got time."

"I guess you do, and I'm the one who suggested getting out this elaborate board." She set the box on the floor. "Let me get a dust rag." She took one from her stash in the kitchen, dampened it and returned to wipe off the box. "I was a freshman on a basketball scholarship when a smooth talker came along and saw me play."

"Then what?"

"He talked me into leaving school and going to Europe to compete over there."

"Oh, no."

"Oh, yes." She opened the box and lifted out the board inlaid with blond and dark wood squares. The hand-carved pieces were tucked inside drawers underneath, dark in one, light in the other.

"I'll take that." Lucky laid it gently on the ottoman. "Looks like it cost a lot."

"Not half as much as that decision. He said he had contacts and could get me a good deal." She stood. "He had contacts but the deal was less than stellar."

"Could you have left?"

"Sure, but that would be admitting I'd made a mistake, that I'd given up my scholarship for a mirage." And she'd been in love.

Empathy shone in his green eyes. "You were young."

"And eager to see the world. That part was terrific, and I have him to thank for a ton of great memories."

"That's a good way to think of it."

"It keeps me from blaming myself for being so gullible. I wanted to believe I could make a bundle and buy my parents a new house. Instead I got three chess sets — one for me, one for my brother and one for my folks."

"Your whole family plays?"

"We sure do. Mom and Dad taught my brother first, since he's four years older than me, and then he taught me. We had an old plastic set that was missing several pieces. We used corks and bottle caps."

"I feel honored you invited me to share this heirloom with you."

"I don't think it qualifies as an heirloom yet. It's only about six years old." She pulled out a velvet-lined drawer and began taking out pieces.

"It's not the age that matters, it's the potential to be passed on." He opened the other drawer. "This chess set has heirloom written all over it."

"I suppose you're right. My brother's kids are already arguing about who gets his."

"See? And you can pass this on to your...." He trailed off. "The next generation."

"Nice save." She smiled at him. "I do hope to have a couple of kids someday, but I'm in catch-up mode after that whoopsie."

"Understood. No rush."

"Absolutely." As she settled into the red chair with a sigh of pleasure her gaze collided with his. Yearning gleamed in those green eyes.

Desire stirred, warm and tempting. She should look away. But it had been a long time since

a man had looked at her like that. She'd allow
herself to enjoy it a little longer.

5

The heat in Oksana's dark eyes took Lucky's breath away. Good thing they had a massive chess board between them. He could move it, but he was *not* doing that even though her gaze promised it would be well worth his time and effort.

He forced himself to break eye contact and glanced down at the board. "Looks like you'll be white." He didn't sound like his normal self. His voice got tight like this when he was very angry or very aroused.

"We can turn it around," came the breathy reply.

"No need." Giving her the first move suited him. "I'm usually black when I play Rance."

"Okay, then." She lined up her pawns.

He followed her lead, his sensitized fingertips sliding over the satin surface of each piece. The urge to touch her made him shaky. He knocked over the king as he set down the queen.

Get it together, dude. It's only Oksana. You've spent hours alone with her without developing a woody. You can manage a game of chess.

Taking a restorative breath, he risked glancing at her. She wasn't looking back. Instead she'd leaned over the board to put the last pieces in place. Her shirt gaped, revealing plump cleavage and red silk.

He ducked his head, but not before noting how the chair cradled her tush and thighs. Didn't take much imagination to picture her sitting in it wearing nothing but her red bra and panties. He shifted in his seat to relieve the pressure building behind his fly.

Was this a hopeless situation? Should he cut and run? Or likely hobble, considering his current situation. No. He had to get past this, had to calm this unwelcome case of lust or he'd create awkwardness between them that would take weeks to wear off.

Once they started playing, he'd become absorbed in the game. "It's your—"

"Before we start, let's heat some more cider." She stood, putting him at eye level with the vee of her jeans.

He gulped. "Sure. Sounds great." He almost knocked over the chess board in his haste to scramble up and bring his attention back to her face. And her lips. And her eyes.

She headed for the kitchen. "While we warm the cider, we can talk about what's happening here."

"Happening?" It came out as a croak.

"C'mon, Lucky." Grabbing two bottles of cider from the fridge, she opened them and dumped the contents into the pan they'd used earlier. "You're ready to tackle me and I'm wishing you would."

He let out a groan of frustration. "Don't say stuff like that. I'm having enough trouble as it is."

"Me, too." She flicked the knob on the stove. "But it's a bad idea."

"Tell that to my—"

"Can't. I'm too busy talking to its counterpart."

He laughed. Couldn't help it. Only Oksana would come up with that comment. "And what does your *counterpart* have to say?"

"Oh, she's ready to rumble. She told me to lean over so you'd look down my shirt."

He scrubbed a hand over his face. "You're not helping."

"But I will." Turning around, she rested her hips against the counter and crossed her arms over her chest. "I'll take a wild guess I'm the best employee you've ever had."

"Yes, ma'am. Hands down." And he wanted his hands down her jeans, damn it. Why did she have to be so sexy all of a sudden?

"This is the best job I've ever had, especially since I can take online classes when I'm not working. Until now I've been able to hide the fact I have a crush on you."

"Since when?" That was news.

"Day one."

Bigger news. "Is that why you took the job?"

"No, but it was a factor. You tick all the boxes. You're a highly literate cowboy. That combo really does it for me. And you're damned good-looking. Those green eyes are killer."

Heat crept up from his collar. "I can't take credit for any of that."

"You didn't have to develop a love of books."

"It would have been hard not to. Mom's done her best to pass that trait on to all of us." He could tell her that much without giving away the family secret. "But I'm the only one who begged to hang out at this bookstore when I was a kid."

"I would have, too, except we didn't have money for books. I spent all my spare time at the library."

He nodded. "I also went there a lot. That's where you get the smell of old books."

"I know! Nothing like it. Have you ever thought of having a rare books section?"

"Considered it, but a few shelves of them wouldn't give you the same effect." He checked the stove. "Cider's steaming."

"Oh!" She whirled around and turned off the heat. "Thanks."

"Welcome." Their little chat had cooled him down a bit. Maybe he'd be okay for the chess game.

She poured cider into the freshly washed mugs and handed him one. "I got off topic, so let me finish before we sit down again."

"Okay."

"Because I like you so much and wouldn't mind staying in Wagon Train, I checked with the school system about employment prospects."

His heart thumped faster. She'd always been in the *leaving town* category. "And?"

"Bleak. Both counselors on staff, primary school and secondary, plan to stay until they retire, which is twenty years in one case and fifteen in the other."

"Ouch." He shared her disappointment, and yet...relief figured in there somewhere. He liked her, but he was still sitting on that damn fence. "Plans change." Although with Wagon Train teachers, not so much.

"I mentioned that. The superintendent offered to add me to a long waiting list of qualified applicants willing to leave their current job to work here."

"Wow. I didn't know we were so popular. Good thing Ella and Faye got on when they did."

"Timing is everything. Evidently the national award the district won last fall caught people's attention."

"Enough that they'd pull up stakes?"

"Why not? Cozy little town, excellent pay and a population that supports education by passing generous bond measures."

"We are good about that. Mom and the Wenches go door-to-door when those votes come up."

"And your superintendent is grateful. He gives community leaders and the *Sentinel* a lot of credit for the district's success."

"It's all good news, except for your odds of getting hired here." Yeah, he was sad for her. She clearly wanted to find a way to live in Wagon Train and her happiness mattered to him.

"He told me, in a nice way, that I was barking up the wrong tree. I saw no reason to tell you before, but now...."

He let out a breath. "I'm glad you did."

"If it was only a physical attraction, then maybe we could justify it. Live for the moment and walk away."

"That's not me." He held her gaze. "And I have trouble believing that's you."

"Not even slightly." She smiled, but her eyes held only disappointment. "Now that we've talked it to death, are you cooled off? Because I sure am."

"Cooled off and slightly depressed. I didn't realize how attached you've become to... the town." And him, but the less they referenced that the better.

"Tough not to. I even saw myself working at the shop during my summer breaks, although I can't imagine doing that and not living upstairs."

"I could have let you keep it as a part-timer. I would've had to charge you something, but it wouldn't have been much." He shrugged. "None of which matters, although I have trouble picturing anyone else living there. I'll have to get over that."

"Make sure they give you a ride to the Buffalo."

He grimaced. "Right." He gestured toward the chess board. "Come on, Jones. Cider's cooling off, too. Let's do this thing."

"Might as well." She took her seat and put her mug of cider on top of the electric fireplace. "I doubt we'll get in too much trouble sitting on opposite sides of this ginormous board."

He kept his response to himself as he settled into the other chair. She was kidding herself if she believed they had this attraction under control.

Their discussion had temporarily derailed his urges, but all he had to do was look at her and his body warmed. The longer he stayed in this apartment, the more likely he'd crack.

One game. Then he was outta there.

6

Oksana had prepared herself for a tough match and Lucky had given her one. Whenever she thought she had him on the ropes, he'd come up with a move she hadn't anticipated and lived to fight on.

But he wasn't having any luck outsmarting her, either. More than once he'd sworn under his breath as she'd wiggled out of a jam. Made her smile.

Got her hot, too. Like now, when he was hunched over the board, a frown of concentration drawing his dark brows together. She'd put him in a spot. He had one way out. Any other move and he was toast.

He gripped his denim-clad knee with one hand while he debated his next move. His other hand was in constant motion, hovering above one piece after another.

He had strong hands, a necessity if he was required to split firewood for his cabin and helpful when he needed to haul a heavy chair up a long flight of stairs. She'd fantasized that those hands could be gentle, too, although she had little basis for that theory.

A few times he'd laid his hand on her shoulder to get her attention. Nothing sexual intended, yet she'd stored away each precious moment, along with every instance when she'd touched him.

Her fingertips retained the memory of each contact, the flex of his muscled forearm when she'd stopped him from shelving a book in the wrong place, the tingle of a high-five when they'd finished the inventory chore and the silky texture of his hair when she'd plucked out a piece of shredded packing material .

He had fabulous hair. She longed to reach across and comb it back from his forehead.

Shoving it back with a murmur of impatience, he made his move. The wrong one.

"Are you sure you want to do that?"

"Yes." He ran a finger over his beard. "I... oh, damn."

She cornered his king. "Checkmate."

"Hell's bells! Can't believe I didn't see that." He glanced up, a gleam of respect in his emerald eyes. "Well done."

"Thank you. You don't make many mistakes."

"That was a doozy, though." Rising from his chair, he stepped away from the board. "Long game. I should probably take that generous offer of stew and head on down to Bret and Gil's shop."

Her heart stuttered. It was over. He was ending this unexpected and thrillingly sexy interlude. A sharp jab of disappointment stole her breath. "Do you..." She gulped for air. "Do you think it's safe to drive?"

"Probably. The wind's let up."

Yes, it had. She'd been so focused on him she hadn't noticed the silence outside. The sound of a giant throwing gravel at the window had stopped. But maybe his truck was buried in snow.

She stood. "Better check on your truck and make sure you can get out."

"That's why we have a snow shovel in the storeroom, but yeah, I'd rather not have to use it."

He would shovel himself out if necessary, though. His firm tone told her he'd settled on his next step. No waffling. He clattered down the stairs.

The closeness they'd shared this afternoon was already evaporating. Once he drove away, it would be gone for good. The blizzard had offered her a tantalizing and frustrating glimpse of what they could have meant to each other if they'd been dealt a different hand.

Thanks a lot, Mother Nature. She picked up the empty mugs and her gaze fell on the red chair. Wait a minute. Wait a damn minute.

Mother Nature wasn't the only one involved in this caper. Lucky wouldn't have been caught in a blizzard if he'd chosen to bring the chair into town on Monday after the storm cleared. Rance had suggested waiting, but he hadn't taken his brother's advice. Why not?

Evidently he'd worked himself into a lather about this surprise gift he'd been seeking for months and had finally found and purchased. Delaying the gratification of seeing her reaction hadn't been an option.

Instead he'd put aside his normal common sense and charged into the teeth of an impending blizzard. He'd acted out of character and single-handedly created this situation. Before she gave him the stew, she wanted some answers.

"Drifts aren't too bad," he called out over the thud of his boots on the stairs. "My four-wheel drive should handle it." He came through the door wearing his hat and his unbuttoned coat. "Still snowing heavily, but..." He caught sight of her standing beside the chair and paused. "What's up?"

"Can you tell me again why you bought this?"

He looked confused. "To replace the crappy one." He gestured to the threadbare and wobbly excuse for an easy chair. "You deserved better than this piece of junk."

"Because I'm the best employee you've ever had?"

"Well, that, and because... I like you. I wanted to do something nice for you."

"But why take all the extra time and trouble to get a red one? A brown chair like this would have been a perfectly nice replacement. Or a dark green one. Or a neutral tan that goes with everything. I'll bet those are relatively easy to find."

"Oh, they are. I agree that would have been an improvement, but I know how much you love red. Why wouldn't I hold out for one in your favorite color?"

"Lucky, that's a little over the top, even for someone as generous as you, and I really can't figure out—"

"Okay, what's with the third degree?"

"Why were you hell-bent on bringing it to me today?"

"It was already in the truck."

"Agreed, but you were *at the ranch*, a minute or two away from the safety of your cabin with a *snowstorm* bearing down on you."

"I thought I could beat it."

"Really? How long have you lived here?"

"So I was wrong! So I miscalculated! So what?"

"Taking it to your cabin for safekeeping was the sensible thing to do, the typical Lucky McLintock move. But no, you had to barrel into town, knowing you might get stuck overnight and be forced to scramble for a place to stay. That's not how you normally operate."

He glanced away and massaged the back of his neck. Then he sighed and met her gaze. "I honestly can't explain it except that I've been looking for the right chair for so long and red wasn't showing up, and I was excited to finally get exactly what I had in mind. I knew you'd love it and I..." He shrugged. "I couldn't wait to see the look on your face."

She melted. Then she wanted to cry. He was in love with her, poor sap, and he didn't know it. Worse yet, she was in love with him and hadn't been willing to admit that, either.

What a pair. She took a shaky breath. "That's extremely sweet of you. I do love the chair and I'm glad you were so excited that you had to bring it to me today. Because of that, we've had a very special afternoon."

"Yes, we have." His voice sounded a little rusty.

"I'll get your stew." She walked toward the kitchen.

"Want me to put the chess pieces back in the drawers?"

"Just leave it as is, please. I want to savor my victory for a little while."

"You play really well."

"Thanks. So do you." She dished a large portion of stew into a glass container and snapped on the lid. He hadn't suggested they play again sometime, had he? She certainly wouldn't.

Turning around, she almost bumped into him. She glanced up to find remorse clouding his eyes.

"I should have taken the chair to my cabin." He cleared his throat. "I don't regret spending time with you today, but I'm afraid I've caused a problem between us."

"I can deal with it if you can." Her crazy heart started going nuts. He was so close. And so beautiful.

"But if I hadn't brought the chair today, we wouldn't have anything to deal with."

"That's where you're wrong." She dredged up a smile. "We just wouldn't have acknowledged it. Now we have. Maybe that's better."

"If you say so."

"We don't ever have to speak of it again, though."

He nodded. "Understood."

"But…" Did she dare? Oh, hell, it was now or never. "Since this is it, and we're putting everything behind us, would you… kiss me before you go?"

He sucked in a breath and light flared in his eyes.

When he didn't reply, she backpedaled. "Never mind. It's probably a terrible—"

"Not terrible." His words slid over her like velvet. Taking the bowl of stew, he reached around her and set it on the counter. He put his hat there, too. "I've been wanting to do this for a long, long time."

"Longer than you've been looking for that chair?" Her voice squeaked at the end.

"Ever since you interviewed for the job." Cupping her face in his warm hands, he lowered his head and brushed his mouth over hers.

Her heart pounded so fast and loud she nearly blacked out. His lips touched down again, gently melding with hers. The softness of his beard against her skin was unexpectedly erotic. She forgot to breathe as he increased the pressure, coaxing her mouth to open to him.

She was extremely coaxable. Burying her fingers in his thick hair, she pulled him closer with a moan of pleasure. One of them got tongues involved. Might have been her, but he was on board with it.

What had begun as a meeting of mouths soon escalated to full-body contact. She abandoned the pleasure of his hair for the thrill of sliding her arms inside his shearling jacket and hugging him like there was no tomorrow. Because, sadly, that was true.

As if he had the same idea, he cupped her ass in those strong hands of his and brought her in tight, tight enough to discover exactly what was going on with him. She wiggled to let him know she got the message.

He groaned in response. Then he slowly peeled himself from her needy body and backed away, stumbling once. Breathing hard, he stared at her. "I have to leave."

She nodded, a hand pressed to her thundering heart.

He continued edging toward the door, hatless. And stew-less.

"Wait!"

"Oh, yeah." He blinked, swiped a hand over his head. "My hat."

"And the stew."

She managed to retrieve both and take them to him without dropping anything. She made the transfer quickly and stepped away. "See you."

"Thanks." He still looked like a man struck by lightning.

She dragged in a breath. "Are you safe to drive?"

"Yes, ma'am." His chest heaved and he turned away. He took the stairs like a drunk being chased by a grizzly, but there was no crash. The bell hanging from the front doorknob jingled. "Lock up after me!" he called out.

"I will!" Locking the shop was easy, a simple twist of the deadbolt. But her heart would remain wide open. And Lucky McLintock had the only key.

7

After pulling on his gloves, Lucky welcomed the physical challenge of getting his truck door free of the ice holding it shut. If he could magically transport himself back home, he'd probably spend the evening splitting enough firewood to last him the rest of the winter.

So what if it was still snowing? The heat generated by Oksana's kiss would last through the night, maybe through the following week. He was on fire with no way to extinguish the flames.

Once the door popped open, he grabbed a scraper from the console, cleared the driver's side of the windshield and the driver's side window. Good enough for half a mile. He hopped in.

Adrenaline still pumped through his system, making him clumsy as he tried to shove the key in the ignition. He had energy to spare but his fine motor skills sucked. Good thing nobody else would be on the road.

He almost drove away and left the container of stew in the snowdrift where he'd set it while he wrestled with the iced-over door. Getting back out, he retrieved the stew and put it on the floor of the passenger side.

Four-wheel drive got him out of the parking space and he headed down the middle of the deserted street, windshield wipers flapping. His were the only tire tracks as he plowed through a layer of snow, spraying it towards the gutters. Kind of pretty when the plumes caught the glow from the streetlamps lining the sidewalk.

Oksana would have enjoyed seeing it. She noticed things like that. *Oksana.* Talk about a major miscalculation. What the hell had he been thinking? That it would be a sweet and tender moment before they closed the book on what might have been?

Yeah, that's exactly what he'd been thinking — a soulful, restrained kiss between two people in a sad G-rated movie with soft violins playing in the background. Instead it became two people in a lusty lip-lock starring in an X-rated movie with loud drums beating frantically in the background.

He could still taste her, still feel her body plastered against his. His heart continued to pound like those drums in the X-rated soundtrack and his cock was very unhappy with the outcome of that lollapalooza of a kiss. What a mess.

They had the rest of the weekend to process what had happened, but that likely wasn't long enough. He could give her a week off to go visit her parents, but that made no sense. She'd just seen them during the week between Christmas and New Year's.

And she'd miss the wedding if she left now, an event she was really looking forward to. Or had been. He might have ruined that for her, too. No matter which way he cut this thick cake of misery, he ended up with all the blame on his plate.

She was right — the red chair had been a ridiculous extravagance. Trent's assumption that he'd bought it for a girlfriend was spot on. Too bad that motivation hadn't been obvious to *him* until Oksana had pointed it out.

The faint glow of a security light inside McLintock Metalworks guided him to the parking area in front of his brothers' shop. Rivet wouldn't be there to greet him. Gil and Faye kept the cat on weekends these days since Bret and Molly had their hands full with a toddler and a baby.

After switching off the engine, he searched through the keys on his ring to locate the one for the shop. He'd only used it once, about a month ago, when Bret had asked him to check on whether the furnace was working since they'd had some issues. Fortunately for the landlord's pocketbook it had been fine.

The thermostat would be turned down for the weekend, so he'd leave some cash to cover the extra electricity he'd use tonight. Gripping the key between his gloved fingers, he picked up the stew and stepped out into a deepfreeze.

Maybe Oksana's kiss was wearing off, because he shivered. Time to get inside, turn up the heat and warm the stew. If he'd been thinking, he would have grabbed a book on his way out since he'd have no other source of entertainment.

He hadn't been thinking, though. Would Bret or Gil have a book stashed somewhere in that tiny apartment? He'd soon find out.

Jabbing the key in the lock, he put some force into twisting it. Eventually the lock clicked. He shoved the door open, walked in and closed it with a sigh of relief.

Uh-oh. In the glow from the security light, he could see his breath. Why could he see his breath? Flipping a switch near the door, he hotfooted it to the thermostat on the back wall.

Turned off? What the hell? Using his teeth to remove his right glove, he laid it on the computer desk and set the container of stew on the glove so it wouldn't leave a ring. He dropped the keys on the lid, pulled out his phone and called Gil.

His brother answered right away. "Hey, bro."

"Did you know the heat's turned off in your shop?"

"I do know that, but why are you there?"

"It's a long story, but aren't you worried about your pipes burst—"

"Yes, and it's handled. The furnace went belly-up around three yesterday. We notified Ed, and the soonest he could get somebody to look at it was Monday, so he asked us to drain the pipes and close up."

"Oh."

"What's your long story about why you're there?"

"I, um, bought a chair for the bookstore while I was in Missoula and thought I could deliver it and make it back to the ranch." He started to shiver again. Damn cold in here.

"And since you didn't, you were hoping to crash at the shop?"

"Yeah, but—"

"How about the B&B? I'll bet Mrs. J can find a place for you."

"I'm sure she can, too." She absolutely would. She'd offered him the Victorian settee in her library, which would muck up the room where she normally gave her guests wine in the evening and coffee in the morning, both in front of a cheerful fire. He wasn't interrupting that program because he'd screwed up.

"If for some reason she can't, you're welcome to take the sheets, blankets and pillows to the bookstore. I know you hate sleeping on the floor, but at least you won't freeze to death. They're predicting minus fifty tonight. Don't be stupid."

"I won't." Gil's warning was way too late. He'd boarded the stupid train some time ago and he couldn't seem to get off.

"Knowing Oksana, she'll take pity on you and give you something to eat."

"Probably." The less said about that, the better. "Hey, I'm sorry about the furnace. I know it'll be Ed's expense, not yours, but will it impact the business?"

"No telling, but he'll do his best. He's been an excellent landlord, so we'll just go with the flow."

"Good plan."

"Hey, at least you got our groomsmen duds before the blizzard hit. Thanks for taking point on that project."

"Happy to." He clenched his teeth to keep them from chattering.

"Unfortunately, Dallas's family won't make it tomorrow night as planned. They're rescheduled for Monday. And we're supposed to have sunny skies for the fourteenth, just what Angie asked for."

"That's g-good."

"Yikes, I need to let you go. Get out of that shop and find yourself somewhere warm."

"Thanks, I'll d-do that." He disconnected, tucked the phone away and picked up his keys. Good thing he'd left them on the stew or he would have forgotten it again.

Tucking it under his arm, he put the glove on his numb fingers and barreled toward the door. Wait. He'd been offered bedding. But he needed to get warm.

Heated truck cab first. Then he could think straight. Hypothermia was a thing. He'd never experienced it. Heard stories, though.

He didn't lock the shop. He would after he got the bedding. He scrambled into the truck like a toddler seeking his mother's lap. He was that cold.

Slamming the door, he started the truck. It dinged in protest because he hadn't fastened his seat belt. "Later, later." He crossed his arms over his chest and waited for the shivers to subside.

Eventually, thanks to the truck's heater blasting into the small space, he thawed out enough to take stock of his situation. He only had one option, and he didn't like it. Although he knew plenty of folks in Wagon Train, he didn't know any well enough to invite himself into their home for the night.

Especially because he'd put himself in this embarrassing, highly avoidable position. He couldn't even claim he'd done it for Oksana. She would have been fine getting her chair on Monday.

She was also the only person who knew why he'd acted like an idiot and for some reason she'd forgiven him. Maybe because he wrote her paycheck every month, but he didn't really believe that. She had feelings for him.

That made it tougher to call and confess that his only option was a bedroll on the floor of the bookstore. He'd eat the stew cold and make himself coffee in the pot they kept downstairs. He'd use the bathroom in the back of the store.

Resigned to his fate, he took out his phone. It rang before he could make the call. Oksana.

And bam, the adrenaline rush was back with a vengeance. "I was just going to call you, but you beat me to it."

"Are you okay down there? I told myself you must be or I would have heard from you, but finally I had to make sure. How's the shop working out?"

"I'm not in the shop. I'm parked in front of it with the motor running."

"Why are—"

"The furnace is out." He quickly explained the problem.

"Then you can't stay there."

"Nope. Gil told me to take the sheets and blankets so I'm going back in to get them."

"You're not sleeping in the truck!"

"I'd run out of gas. I'll have to make a bedroll on the floor of the bookstore. I won't need to bother you for anything. Just pretend—"

"That you're not even here? Are you insane?"

"That's up for debate. I'm sorry about this, Oksana. I've been a pain in the rear, but once we get through this night, we can start over."

Silence. But she was still there, judging from the faint sound of her breathing.

He waited. Still nothing. "You're ticked and I don't blame you. If I had any other—"

"I don't want to start over."

"What?"

"I don't even think it's possible, now that we've taken off our blinders and you've had your tongue in my mouth. And vice-versa."

He groaned as his cock responded. "I thought we agreed to—"

"We did! I was working on it! And now you're coming back with this lame idea of a bedroll downstairs. How about sharing the queen bed upstairs? How about that?"

"We can't." His buddy in his Jockeys had the opposite opinion.

"We most certainly can, and I want to."

"Even if I thought it was a great idea, which I don't...." He was such a liar. "There's the matter of condoms."

"Not a problem. I have some."

He gulped. "I see." His hand shook as he reached over and turned down the heat in the cab. Five minutes ago he'd thought he'd never get warm again. Now he had to unbutton his jacket.

"I've had my own supply ever since I was old enough to have sex. My folks made sure my brother and I were educated and prepared."

It was his turn to stare at his phone without talking.

"You're probably worried about our working relationship."

"I am."

"But that's already jacked up."

"Because of me. My actions. I take full responsibility for the current awkward situation and I say we can still fix it."

"I agree, but not by avoiding the issue. That guarantees we'll be weird around each other. We need to meet this head on and have sex to release the tension."

"Just one time?" Whoops. Looked like he'd just taken a step down a slippery slope.

"As many times as we want. For tonight only."

As sweat trickled down his spine, he turned the heater down another notch. "In other words, a one-night stand."

"Basically, I guess. I've never had one. Are there rules?"

"Don't ask me. I've never had one, either. I think usually it's between two people who've just met and they never plan to see each other again."

"Then we don't fit the profile, but it doesn't matter. We can just set a one-night limit. And nobody needs to know but us."

He lowered the heat until it was damn near off. "That's not so easy in a small town."

"But not impossible. I'm from a small town, too, and I know a golden opportunity when it's staring me in the face. Does anyone in your family know you have a crush on me?"

"How could they? I wouldn't admit it to myself."

"How about Gil's suggestion to bring a bedroll down here? Any indication he thought something might happen between us?"

"None. He even said you might take pity on me and give me some food."

"Then you need to haul that bedding down here."

"I do?"

"Absolutely. And thank him profusely when you return it washed and carefully folded, just as you would if you'd actually used it."

"I'm getting the picture. Nobody thinks of me as a one-night-stand type."

"Bingo. Everyone thinks of you as the quiet, responsible type, which you are ninety-nine percent of the time."

"They'll expect me to spend the night in a bedroll downstairs."

"But instead...." She didn't finish the sentence.

She didn't have to. He already had a raging case of lust that blocked out any sense of responsibility he had left. "I'll be there in five minutes."

8

Five minutes? Oksana disconnected, tossed down the phone and raced to the bathroom, yanking the scrunchie from her hair as she ran. *No time, no time, no time.*

Swishing mouthwash, she brushed her hair until it crackled with static electricity. Then she quickly shucked her clothes.

She'd always hated the awkward undressing phase, but greeting him naked was a bit much. What should she wear?

Like she had a choice. Her buffalo plaid PJs were in the wash, so her red polka dot ones would have to do. At least they were easy on, easy off. She grabbed them from the middle drawer of her dresser and shoved her feet through the elastic cuffs of the pants.

As she pulled the top over her fly-away hair, the bell on the front door jingled. She gasped. Then she choked. And launched into the mother of all coughing fits.

"Oksana?" He pounded up the stairs. "Are you okay?" Charging through the door, he put the container of stew on the floor and headed for her, his eyes dark with worry. "Let me—"

"No!" She managed a strangled protest as she backed away and waved him off. So much for a seductive beginning.

"Water?"

She nodded in between coughs. Tears blurred her view of him and she wiped them away, needing to confirm that he was here. In her space. And once she stopped this ridiculous coughing....

He brought over a glass of water and handed it to her. "Just sip it."

The tenderness in his voice created a heat wave that traveled from the roots of her hair to the tips of her bare toes. She tightened her fingers on the glass so she wouldn't spill water on herself.

He stood without moving, watching her closely as she slowly drank it. When it was gone, she carefully inhaled.

"Better?"

"Uh-huh." She itched to grab him, but her throat still tickled and she was holding a stupid glass.

He smiled and began unbuttoning his jacket. "I was prepared to do the Heimlich."

This was happening. "I could tell." She followed his progress down the row of leather buttons. "You had that Heimlich look in your eye." When he tossed the jacket on the old chair, she began to quiver. The glass had to go. "Let me just set this down."

"Here, I'll take—"

"Take *me*." The glass thunked to the floor as she hurled herself into his arms, knocking off his hat.

"Yes, ma'am." His hot mouth found hers. Cupping her tush, he hoisted her up and carried her the short distance to the bed.

Damn, he was strong. He laid her crossways on the bed and followed her down, the ridge of his fly wedged right where she wanted it. She moaned and wrapped her legs around his hips, tightening the connection.

Hello. That felt like the beginning of—

"Loosen up, pretty lady." His warm breath caressed her cheek as he rocked forward. "Give me room."

Oh, yeah, she could do that. She relaxed her grip so he could keep pushing right *there.* He'd found the magic in two seconds flat. In no time she came apart, gasping, crying out, and finally giggling.

Braced on his forearms, he gave her a slow smile. "Better?" Clearly he was pleased with himself, even a little cocky.

She rarely saw that side of him. What fun. "You didn't even have to take off your clothes!"

"Figured if I took time for that, I'd miss the party."

"Just so you know, that kind of instant reaction is highly unusual for me. I must have been really keyed up."

"I noticed."

"You, on the other hand, are one cool customer, keeping it together while you helped me out."

"I'm not as cool and collected as you think." He gave her a nudge. "If you don't mind, I'd like to try it without the jeans."

"I could go for that."

"Then stay put while I get rid of a few things." He dropped a quick kiss on her mouth and levered himself off the bed.

"Can I watch?"

"Be my guest."

She sat up, her feet dangling over the edge of the mattress. "It's not every day a man strips down in this apartment."

"I used to do it all the time." He toed off his boots while he undid the buttons on his shirt, revealing a white T-shirt stretched across his muscular chest.

"True." She could be happy just being allowed to watch him breathe. To think he'd lived here, cooked in that kitchen, slept in this... wait. He might also have slept *with* someone in this bed.

"I did not." He balled up his shirt and pitched it in the direction of the old chair.

"What?"

"Bring dates here." Leaning over, he pulled off his socks. "Let alone romp around in that rickety bed with them." Reaching for the back of his T-shirt, he tugged it over his head and sent it sailing toward the chair, too.

"It's not that rickety and I wasn't thinking about that." And she certainly wasn't when she was busy admiring the way his dark chest hair defined territory just waiting to be explored.

"Maybe not, but you got a little pucker on your forehead right after I reminded you I used to live in this apartment. It's a logical leap."

"Okay, I did think about it. You even have a dimmer switch on the wall to create atmosphere."

"The previous owner installed it and I've never had a need for atmosphere."

"But this is such a cozy place. Seems perfect for entertaining a girlfriend. Why didn't you?"

"I guess because I never found someone who thought it was awesome living over a bookstore."

"How's that possible? Living over a bookstore is fabulous!"

"Looks like I found that someone." He flashed her a smile.

And her heart stumbled. They'd made a deal — one night and one night only. Was he already dreaming of a different scenario? "Lucky, I—"

"Hey." His voice was gentle. "That was a throwaway line. Don't go reading too much into it."

"If I thought for one minute that I'd break your—"

"Bed? Now that you mention it, that could happen, and if it does, it's my fault, not yours. The mattress is fine but the bed frame's always been dicey. I have my doubts it'll stand up to what I have in mind."

She picked up her cue. "Now you're just bragging." And she loved it when he did.

"I'll let you be the judge of that." He shucked his jeans and briefs in one fluid motion.

Her gulp was loud and involuntary. The man clearly had bragging rights.

"Will I do?" The sparkle of confidence in his green eyes was even sexier than his amazing package.

He'd likely heard her gulp. "The visual is definitely promising. Come on over."

He hesitated. "First tell me where the—"

"Oh! In the cabinet under the bathroom sink." She hopped off the bed. "Sorry. I didn't think to pull them out. I'll get them." But before he put on one of those raincoats, she wanted to touch him all over, some places more than others.

"I'll fetch 'em." He took her by the shoulders, halting her in her tracks. Then he dipped his head. "While you get out of those polka dots." Claiming her lips in a searing kiss, he held her firmly in place and thoroughly ravished her mouth.

His grip of steel had to be on purpose. Maybe he was ready to explode like she'd been minutes ago. She could get away with being fast out of the gate, but guys generally had a different attitude toward orgasms.

Releasing her, he turned away. "Be right back."

She doubted it. If she'd guessed right about his fear of coming too fast, he'd suit up while he was in there. "I'll be waiting." Hurrying over to the wall switch by the door, she dimmed the lights.

Men were visual creatures. He might maintain control more easily if he couldn't see as well.

She took off her PJs and left them next to the bed so they were handy. Lucky didn't strike her as the type to walk around naked when he was staying with a woman.

Pulling back the covers, she got in on the apartment-door side, which made it convenient for him to climb in on the other side when he came out of the bathroom. The sheets were cold, but they'd warm up once the action started.

She wiggled with excitement and anticipation. Clearly he wanted this as much as she did. She'd viewed the physical evidence. But it was their first time together. The earlier episode didn't really count.

He was justifiably nervous that after months of abstinence, he wouldn't provide the stellar experience he longed to give her. Thankfully she wasn't a dewy-eyed virgin. She couldn't wait to help him with the process.

9

Lucky's hands shook as he snapped on the condom. Oksana kept the apartment on the cool side to save on electricity, the same as he had when he'd lived here. He should be shivering. Instead, the blast furnace in his loins kept his naked self quite toasty.

All the way from Bret and Gil's shop he'd told himself to take it easy and not behave like a rutting bull moose when he arrived at the apartment. Or worse, a sixteen-year-old virgin. Although he'd been concerned about her coughing fit, a part of him, the section behind his fly, had been grateful for the temporary distraction.

But once she'd begun to recover, he'd zeroed in on those polka-dot pajamas. She was coughing less, but whenever she did, those polka-dots over her breasts danced. No red bra under there. Likely no red panties under the polka-dot bottoms, either.

She'd provided him with easy access to paradise. Both of those items would come off in a flash. He'd been poised for action when she'd launched herself at him, presenting him with an armful of soft cotton and hot woman.

Good thing she'd been ready to rumble or he'd never have made her come without coming himself. Now he was looking for a similar result and he had serious doubts about his staying power. Face it, he had doubts about the whole program.

Until today, he'd kept his volcano of need dormant for eighteen effing months. So had she. Would one night of hot sex send the flow of lava back underground?

That was crazy logic and he'd been out of his mind to buy into it. But he had, and now there was no turning back. All he could do was love the hell out of her and pray she was right. Loving the hell out of her required lasting more than six seconds, though.

"Did you fall in?"

That made him laugh. It was so her. "I had trouble with the wrapper." He turned out the bathroom light and walked into the soft glow of twilight. "I see you made use of the dimmer switch."

She lay under a mound of covers on the far side of the bed. "I did." She propped her head on her hand and gazed at him. "Sorry about the wrapper. Guess that's not your brand, after all."

That short-circuited any brain cells still functioning. "You bought those for *me*?"

"No! Not intentionally, anyway." She sat up and the covers fell away. "I needed some because my others had expired. The clerk recommended those."

"Oh." He'd lost interest in the conversation. The rise and fall of her tempting breasts held way more appeal than the subject of condom purchases.

Saliva pooled in his mouth as he approached the bed.

Evidently she wanted to give him the whole story. "I hadn't bought any in ages so I asked the clerk what was popular."

"Ages?" He caught that significant word as he pulled back the covers. That might explain why she'd been on fire earlier. Long dry spell.

"School." She scooted under the covers again. "It takes up—"

"But you made time tonight." For which he thanked the blizzard as he climbed in. The bed creaked under his weight, and then he stretched out on warm sheets. She'd done him that favor.

"Tonight's special."

"Sure is." He reached for her, encountering satin skin that delivered an urgent message to his cock. Sliding his hand around her waist, he put pressure on the small of her back. "You should come over here." He tugged her closer. "Someone warmed the sheets on this side."

"I wonder who that was." She took his suggestion and snuggled against him.

Full body contact nearly put him over the edge. No time to waste. With a strangled groan, he rolled her to her back. The covers slid off his shoulders as he rose above her with only one goal in mind. He managed a husky *thank you* before burying his cock deep.

Pleasure hit him with such force he saw stars. The breath hissed through his clenched teeth and he squeezed his eyes shut while he fought to keep his climax at bay.

Lying very still beneath him, she stroked his back. "For what it's worth, I don't care if you come."

"I do."

"Then maybe I can help."

Slowly he opened his eyes. Despite the shadow he created as he loomed over her, he could tell she was looking up at him, her expression endearingly earnest. "How?"

"Like this." Pushing her hand between his groin and hers, she wrapped her fingers around the base of his cock.

He sucked in air. "I don't think—"

"Just stay still." She tightened her grip.

Okay, he was done for. He might as well accept the humiliation of... hmmm. The urge to explode receded slightly. She maintained her hold and gradually he felt less and less like a ticking time bomb.

Where had she learned that? But he didn't really want to know.

"Is it working?"

"Uh-huh." He exhaled. "Try letting go."

She released him.

"Wow." He still wanted to come, but he didn't *have* to. Soon, but not this minute. Leaning down, he nibbled on her lips, then kissed his way down the curve of her throat. "You fixed me."

"That's what friends are for."

"The thing is, you feel so darned good." Shifting his weight to his left forearm, he cradled her breast, reveling in the sensation of fondling her. "Everywhere. Too good, I guess."

"So do you." She took a quick breath as her core muscles rippled over his cock.

"Watch it. You'll ruin what you just fixed."

"That wasn't on purpose."

"But I didn't move."

"Maybe we don't have to."

"It'll be more fun if we do." Flattening his palms on the mattress, he pushed up for greater leverage, which gave him a more complete view of the woman lying beneath him.

Holy hell. She was a goddess. How had he missed that? "Oksana, you're... you're stunning."

Her blush was barely visible in the dim light, but he caught it. "You know that, right?"

"Sometimes."

"I hope this is one of those times, because you're so beautiful right now it makes my throat hurt."

Her breath hitched.

"And I want to make you happy." He began to stroke. "I want to make you feel good. Tell me. Tell me how to do that."

"You're doing just fine." As she clutched his hips and rose to meet his thrusts, she began to pant. "Don't... don't change... a thing."

But he did. He couldn't help it. The delicious friction and her gasps of pleasure drove him to pick up the pace. The bed objected, creaking in protest.

But Oksana didn't object. Just the opposite, her cries grew more enthusiastic and her fingers dug into his flexing muscles.

"Good?"

"Yes!"

Ignoring the sounds of the bed, he poured on the steam. His reward was her shout of joy followed by intense contractions that smashed through his resistance. He ran up the white flag.

With a groan torn from deep in his chest, he let go. The dam burst, and for a moment he was blind and deaf to everything but the rush of blood through his veins and the wild beat of his heart.

Gradually his world stopped spinning at the speed of light, his vision cleared and he could breathe again. He gazed down at Oksana, who looked at least as shell-shocked as he felt.

He tried to speak and had to clear his throat before he could get the words out. "What just happened?"

"I'm not sure." She took a shaky breath. "But that was the best sex of my life."

He nodded. "Me, too."

"I thought we might break the bed, though."

"If we do, we do. I'm not letting that slow us down."

"Good. Me, either." She paused. "So, I've been thinking. We've both been in relationships, and the first time you have sex with someone is never the best. Which means..."

"We'll get better."

"I think so. Maybe not, but—"

"I don't see how we can help it. I'll be better, for sure, now that I've taken the edge off. Next time I want more light, if you're okay with that."

"I mostly turned it down for you."

"I figured, and thanks. I didn't need the extra visual stimulation. Without your little trick, no telling how fast I would have come."

"I know you were worried about that, but I wouldn't have cared if you'd lost control."

"You say that, but you wouldn't have just had the best sex of your life."

"Yeah, there's that." She held his gaze. "This could turn out to be one humdinger of a night."

"Yes, ma'am." And then what?

10

"Sex makes me hungry as a bear," Oksana called out as Lucky headed for the bathroom to ditch the condom. "I'm gonna warm up some stew."

"Might as well use what you gave me," he tossed over his shoulder. "I left it by the door."

"Do you want to eat naked or dressed?"

"Dressed. Saves me the worry of potentially dumping hot stew in my lap."

"Gotcha." She didn't envy men for many reasons and that was one of them. Their tender parts were outside their body, where they could be damaged so easily. Recent events made her especially protective of Lucky's tender parts.

After she put on her PJs, she picked up his jeans and briefs and laid them on the bed. What if they actually broke it? How would she explain *that*?

Oh, well. A problem for another day. Crossing to the door, she closed it before she picked up the container of stew and carried it over to the stove. Her body still hummed with the energy generated by good lovemaking.

Sex had always made her hungry, but this time she was starving. Evidently incredible sex made her ravenous.

After dumping the stew into a pan, she took the big pot out of the fridge and ladled more on top of what she'd already put in, just to be sure she had enough in there. For all she knew, sex made him hungry, too and they'd finish off all the stew before the night was over.

"Smells good."

She looked in the direction of the bedroom alcove, where he was zipping up his jeans. He'd put on his socks but not his boots. Smart man. "It'll warm up fast since it was out of the fridge for a while."

"I'm glad you decided we should eat. I didn't think I was that hungry, but I guess I am." Walking over to the chair, he picked up his T-shirt and pulled it over his head. "Aren't your feet cold?"

"Not yet." Taking a wooden spoon from a crock on the counter, she stirred the pot to make sure the stew wasn't sticking to the bottom. "You heated up every inch of me, including my toes."

"Same here. That's why a T-shirt and jeans is all I need right now." He came toward her, a glow in his green eyes. "Do I get to kiss the cook?"

She glanced at the pot on the stove. "Only if I turn that off. Guaranteed I'd let it boil over."

"Then don't turn it off. You said you're hungry." He smiled. "I can wait."

Ah, that smile. She'd always loved it, but framed by his neatly trimmed beard, it was a show-stopper. "I'm glad you kept your beard. I thought for sure you were going to shave it off this summer."

"I almost did. Then you said you liked it."

She blinked. "You kept it because *I* liked it?"

"Uh-huh. Your opinion carries a lot of weight. Anything I can do to help? Maybe slice up some of that bread we used for the toasted cheese?"

Her answer was slow in coming. He'd kept his beard for her? "Yes, bread would be great. Thanks. Might as well warm up more cider, too."

"I'm on it." He moved around the kitchen without hesitation.

Not surprising, but he hadn't been quite so self-assured earlier, before they'd had sexy times. As for her, she was as excited as a kid on Christmas morning. Santa's gifts were usually modest and handmade, but the mystery of something hidden under wrapping paper had thrilled her.

Lucky was definitely a gift. Although she'd worked with him for a year and a half, she'd learned more in the past few hours than she had in eighteen months.

She appreciated the sex for its own sake, but it also revealed so much about this man. He had layers, and discovering what was underneath would be fascinating.

He set the table while she dished up two generous bowls of stew and put them on the bright red placemats she kept there all the time. As a renter she didn't have a lot of leeway for adding color, but she took advantage of every opportunity.

They took their seats and dived in without preamble, making only short comments in between bites of stew. They were both halfway through a second serving before Lucky put down his spoon and sat back. "I haven't gobbled food like that since I was a teenager."

"I was famished." She paused to take a sip from her mug of cider.

"The stew tastes great." Picking up his napkin, he dabbed at his beard. "Is anything stuck there?"

"Nope, you're good."

He glanced at the napkin color. "I guess I know where to come if I ever need to tie a warning flag on the end of a load in my pickup."

She grinned. "Yes, you do."

"Valentine's Day must be your favorite. All that red."

"I think it is, although I'm very fond of Christmas. Valentine's Day must be Angie's favorite, too, since it's her birthday."

"Maybe, but I've always had the impression her birthday takes center stage and Valentine's Day is more of an afterthought. Now it'll be birthday, wedding anniversary, and then Valentine's Day, so it's been moved down a peg."

"Come to think of it, does she wear red much? I can't remember."

"She likes it, but it's not a favorite. I don't think anyone in the world loves it the way you do."

"Santa Claus."

He laughed. "Besides him. Is that what started it?"

"Oh, no. It was Sigourney Weaver."

"No kidding."

"I think I mentioned the nickname I got in school."

He grimaced. "Yeah, you did. Kids can be mean."

"To be fair, my name plus my size had to be irresistible. By fourth grade I was the tallest kid in our elementary school. It was a small school, but still, to tower over everyone, even the sixth-grade boys, was tough to handle."

"Did basketball help at all?"

"That made it worse, especially for those eleven-year-old boys. I was better than any of them. They didn't take that well."

"I suppose they wouldn't. But I don't get how Sigourney Weaver or the color red figure into the story."

"I found a picture of her in a magazine and she had on a red dress. She was a knockout. So tall and proud. Defiant, even. The minute I saw that picture, I decided red would be my signature color."

"Brilliant. Also, you look great in red."

"Fortunately. And after I saw that picture, when I put on red, it was like a shield."

His gaze softened and he let out a sigh. "One you desperately needed."

"Yep. For a while, that was the only color I wanted to wear. My mom pitched in, altering stuff from Goodwill and hitting sales at the fabric store. By fifth grade I'd figured out wearing nothing but red was its own kind of weird, so I dialed it back."

The corners of his mouth tilted up. "Except for your underwear."

"Oh, man, I was so embarrassed when you walked in and saw that."

"And I was so turned on."

"That never occurred to me. I thought you'd be embarrassed, too, so I got them out of sight the minute I had a chance."

"While I was picturing you wearing your red underwear and lounging in your red chair."

"You were, huh?" Her childhood traumas slipped away, replaced by several X-rated adult images. "Want me to model them for you?"

His eyes glittered. "I wouldn't mind."

_11_

Lucky volunteered to busy himself in the kitchen putting away the remaining stew and washing the bowls and mugs while Oksana exchanged her polka-dot PJs for red underwear. He'd promised not to look until she told him to.

But he could hear her over there moving around, opening a drawer, breathing faster than normal. He was breathing faster, too. The dimmer switch had robbed him of detail when they'd made love. Now he'd get to see... everything.

But first she'd indulge his fantasy of lounging in the red chair in her matching underwear. Would he torture himself with that image for the rest of his life? Could be, but he wasn't giving up the opportunity.

Then he'd pay homage to her beautiful body and her even more beautiful soul. He'd guessed at the level of humiliation she'd suffered as a child. Learning how she'd chosen to deal with it had taught him a lot about her resiliency.

She didn't blame those kids for making fun of her. Instead she'd found a way to protect herself. He hated that an idiot had taken advantage of her trusting nature and made her educational goals harder to reach. But she didn't hold a grudge.

Did she totally believe in her awesomeness? Not yet. When he'd asked if she knew she was beautiful, the answer had been *sometimes.* He had one night to change that answer.

Once he'd returned the clean dishes to the cupboard, he had nothing more to do. He used the dishtowel to polish the stainless-steel faucet and sink. Still not a peep from her.

How long could it take to put on a bra and a pair of panties? Why had she opened the closet? And what was the soft thump all about?

"Okay, cowboy." Her voice was low and throaty. "You can look, now."

Her sexy tone and her flirty use of *cowboy* rendered him stiff as a fence post. The lady knew a thing or two about seduction.

Heart pounding, he turned around. And forgot to breathe.

"Will this do?" Her lips, tinted cherry red, curved in a come-hither smile.

When his fried brain couldn't come up with any words, he settled for a nod. No wonder she'd needed more time.

She'd taken the concept of lounging in the chair to a whole new level. Dangling her right leg over the arm, she'd propped the other on the ottoman, her knee slightly bent to the side.

Her open thighs issued a clear invitation, one he was all too ready to accept. But her erotic presentation deserved to be savored, beginning with the sparkly red stilettos on her feet.

Who would've guessed she had them hiding in her closet? Since he hadn't heard the click of heels on the hardwood, she'd put them on after she'd climbed into the chair. She'd moved the chessboard to achieve this pose, so it was... somewhere. He didn't much care about the chessboard's whereabouts.

He had things to do, like staring at her undies, which weren't meant for a day spent in jeans and a T-shirt. The satin and lace pushup bra and thong demanded a low-cut slinky dress, one that matched the stilettos. A Sigourney Weaver dress.

Did she own one? He'd bet she did.

Swallowing the moisture pooling in his mouth, he admired the tempting swell of her breasts above the small but skillfully constructed bits of material and underwire. Then he traveled the path of least resistance as his avid gaze moved steadily lower. And he was there, focused on the epicenter of her display.

The scrap of cloth barely covered the treasure he craved, but it concealed just enough to make him dizzy with lust. Lifting his head, he looked into her eyes. "I..." He paused to suck in air. "I've never wanted anyone so mu—"

"Me, either." She sounded out of breath, too.

Now what? He was shaking with the need to touch her, to claim the prize she'd offered. Could they do it in the chair? Was that crazy? "Maybe if you... or if I..." Never mind. He had no condom.

"I wanted to, but—"

"What?"

"Make love in the chair." She pushed the ottoman aside with her foot and stood on her five-inch heels, bringing her eye to eye with him. "It's too hard."

He choked on a laugh. "That's the damn truth."

"Come on." Grabbing his hand, she tugged him toward the bed, her heels tapping on the floor.

"I'll need—"

"I have one."

"Where?"

"You'll find out."

He stumbled after her, his breathing like an engine about to throw a rod. She'd also folded back the covers before arranging herself in the chair. She'd had a plan, but now she was clearly making it up on the fly.

Kicking off the stilettos, she let go of his hand and climbed onto the mattress, giving him a mind-blowing view of how the red satin thong looked from the back. He was out of his duds in no time.

But he was still missing a vital item. "Where is it?"

Flopping to her back, she spread her arms wide and opened her thighs. "Take a guess."

He groaned and crawled in after her. "You'll be the death of me, woman." But the location was obvious to him, now. Positioning himself right where he'd need to be once he found the little raincoat, he braced himself on his left hand and flipped open the front catch of her bra.

The cups fell away, giving him his first fully lit view of her creamy breasts. No condom, but oh, what he'd found. When he stroked her silken skin with the tips of his fingers, her wine-red nipples tightened, begging for attention.

Driven by a need as old as time, he ignored one powerful urge to satisfy another. Yearning rose hot in his chest as he lowered his head, pulled one sweet bud into his mouth and began to suck.

Her breathing picked up, followed by soft cries of pleasure. Familiar cries. And he got the message. Shifting his weight to one hand, he slipped the other one under her thong. Foil crinkled. He'd found the condom.

But he had something to do before he unwrapped it. Laying it next to her hip, he returned to the spot where she'd hidden it. Her gasp when he pushed his fingers deep told him all he needed to know.

Continuing to draw her plump breast into his mouth, he rhythmically stroked her passion-slick channel. It didn't take long. She came apart, abandoning herself to the flames he'd nurtured, becoming vulnerable in the most intimate of ways. Her openness humbled him. What man could ask for a greater gift?

Easing his hand free, he slid down a little so he could lay his cheek over her heart and listen to its rapid beat. His package wasn't happy pressed against the mattress, but until he opened that packet, it was the safest position. He palmed the condom so he wouldn't lose track of it.

"You... you were supposed to...." She tunneled her fingers through his hair as she slowly got her breath back. "I thought you'd move on to...."

"Got sidetracked."

"But then... you found it, and you still didn't...."

"I had to finish what I'd started." He turned his head and kissed her warm breast. "I hope you didn't mind."

"You know I didn't. And now I want to finish what I started. You must be a powder keg."

"Maybe."

"Where's the condom?"

"In my left hand."

"Good thing it's not lost somewhere under the covers."

"Not a chance." Pushing himself to his knees, he sat back on his heels and suited up while taking in the view of Oksana looking completely ravished. Her bra lay open and her thong was askew. Her dark hair tumbled over the pillow, evidence of how she'd thrashed around at the peak of her climax.

Best of all, her dark eyes glittered as she watched him putting on the condom. When she lifted her gaze to meet his, adrenaline shot through his system. She wanted him. Still. Again. Even though she'd come three times since he'd walked through the door.

"Hold on. I need to help you out."

"Thanks. I've got it." He snapped the condom into place.

"Not with that. With this." Bringing one knee to her chest, she slipped the elastic of the thong over her foot, flashing him in the process. Looked deliberate, too.

Lord have mercy. By the time she'd completed the move a second time and tossed the tiny panties to the floor, he was panting.

She peered at him. "Are you okay?"

"Lady, you just poured gasoline on the fire."

"Did I, now?" She gave him a slow, seductive smile. "And what are you going to do about it, cowboy?"

Planting a palm on either side of her head, he leaned down, his mouth hovering over hers as he paused, the tip of his cock tucked just inside the entrance to paradise. "You're about to find out."

<u>12</u>

Oksana had never seduced a man in her life. Might never do it again. But Lucky brought out the vixen in her.

And the rogue in him. Now he was drawing out the moment, taunting her with the barest of touches in an extremely sensitive spot. She pinched his butt.

"Ow." His warm breath caressed her lips.

"Get on with it. Show me what you've got."

"Glad to." In one glorious move, he filled the aching void with a powerful thrust that lifted her off the mattress. The headboard smacked against the wall and the bed shivered.

Her laughter turned into a moan of pleasure as their intense connection sent joy spreading to every nerve in her body. She dragged in a breath. "Lucky, you're gonna break this bed."

"Don't care." Pulling back, he drove deep again. The headboard banged against the wall a second time. "Do you?"

The fire in his green eyes made her giddy. "Your bed. Your choice."

"You need a new one." And he picked up the pace.

At first the rapid thump of the headboard against the wall brought on giggles. But that quickly changed to wild cries as he turned her inside out. The beat of the bed hitting the wall became a drumroll. Her climax bore down on her... almost there... almost....

"Now."

Rapture bubbled up, coaxing her to let go. Chanting his name, she embraced the tsunami that engulfed her.

He pushed home once more with a triumphant shout. The rhythmic pulse of his orgasm joined hers, followed by the crack and pop of wood splintering.

Gulping for air, he scooped one arm under her shoulders and the other around her waist. "Hang on."

She hugged him tight. For a second the frame held. Then the siderails gave way, the slats clattered to the floor and the box spring and mattress dropped. She and Lucky bounced once but stayed firmly connected.

His breath was still coming fast as he lifted his head and looked down at her. "You okay?"

"Yep." She sucked in air. "You actually broke it."

"Sure did." He chuckled. "Felt great." He propped himself on his forearms and surveyed the damage. "We're not lying flat, though. Was there something under—"

"A box."

"Uh-oh."

"Nothing breakable. Notes and stuff."

"For your classes?"

"No. Something else." Should she tell him? Only her mom knew.

"That sounds private."

"Not really. I just..." She needed a moment to gather her thoughts. "We should probably untangle so we can—"

"Right." His chest heaved. "I'm sorry about the box, though."

"I forgot it was under there. I forgot everything but you."

The gleam returned to his eyes. "Ditto."

"Well, everything but you and the thump of the bed against the wall. That was awesome. A real turn-on. Even the wood cracking added to the thrill. I'm usually not into destruction, but that was fun."

He laughed. "Yeah, it was. Destruction isn't normally my thing, either." He glanced up at the wall. "Fortunately I have touch-up paint downstairs." Then he met her gaze and took a deep breath. "The bed had to go."

"Clearly." She'd studied enough psychology to recognize he was changing, whether he knew it or not.

"I'll smuggle the pieces out of here and take them to the dump."

"Okay, but you'll have to offer some explanation for why you so abruptly got rid of it."

"Termites."

"The ones that chew on beds and leave everything else alone?"

"How about mold? While I was here overnight you mentioned that the bed frame had gray fuzzy stuff growing on it."

"You can use bleach to get rid of that."

"But it's a lot of trouble for a cheap piece of furniture my mom picked up at a yard sale twenty-some years ago. She and I have talked about replacing it with something better, but we never seem to make that happen."

"Then mold it is."

"And we have our story. Short but sweet." He dropped a soft kiss on her mouth. "I'll go take care of the condom and then we'll decide next steps."

"Sounds like a plan." She let go of him and he carefully disengaged.

Making his way off the uneven surface, he stood. "Don't try to move anything until I get back."

"I won't." She sat up. Bits of what looked like particleboard littered the floor. "Watch your step."

"You, too. Maybe you should stay put until I get back."

"Sorry. Helpless female isn't in my repertoire."

He laughed and made his way to the bathroom. "Thanks for the reminder."

Checking the area next to the mattress and box springs, she climbed over the siderail lying on the floor. She had to move it to free her PJs and Lucky's clothes. Then she stepped carefully away from the collapsed bed and walked into the sitting area so she could shake everything.

Lucky came out of the bathroom as she finished putting on her PJs. "I laid your stuff over on the chair." She casually gestured toward it, as if she was unaffected by having a naked and ripped cowboy in her apartment.

She had to work to keep from staring, though. He was the most beautiful man she'd ever seen in person. True, her mental gallery wasn't huge, but it included some handsome guys with decent physiques.

"Thanks." He walked over and picked up his briefs from the pile. "I probably could have planned this episode better. If I'd broken the bed toward the end of the night, we wouldn't be wasting valuable time on cleanup."

"I think the bed was doomed once you mentioned your fantasy about me in the chair."

"I didn't think you'd do it." He pulled on his jeans.

"Now you know better."

"Oh, I've learned a lot, but I still don't have all the pieces. Where did those shoes come from?"

"Paris. They're knock-offs of a famous brand. I can't remember which one."

"Is there a red dress in your closet?"

"Yep. I saw it the same day I bought the shoes and the fancy underwear. That was my only splurge besides the chess sets." She turned and headed for the kitchen. "I'll get a broom and dustpan."

"I'd love to see you wear that outfit."

"You mean tonight?"

"Well, sure, you could model it for me, but I was thinking..." He paused.

She faced him, broom in hand. "What?"

"Never mind. It wouldn't work. I was about to say you should wear it to the Buffalo. For a night out. With me."

Pain shot through her chest. "Nice idea, though."

"Rance said I should take you to dinner in return for your work at the shop. He's right, but—"

"Don't give up on it. Maybe a dinner out would be problematic now, but eventually we could consider it."

"Maybe." He sat in the chair to put on his socks. "I need to get my boots. Can I bring you some from your closet?"

"My Ugg boots, please. Then I don't need socks."

"I'll get 'em." Standing, he padded cautiously over to the closet and pushed back the bi-fold door.

Instead of stooping down for the boots, he reached in, unhooked a hanger from the rod and held it out. "Pretty much how I pictured it. Wondered if it would be sleeveless." His earnest expression as he studied her red dress brought a lump to her throat.

"I like that it's not. The long sleeves mean I can wear it in cold weather, which is important in Montana."

"As long as you have a warm coat when you're outside."

She smiled. "True. My ta-tas would freeze without one."

"Have you worn it since you moved here? Because I think I would have remembered."

"I've never had a reason to."

"What about Marsh and Ella's wedding last August? Why not then?"

"First of all, it's a bit dramatic for a wedding. And it needs those shoes to pull off the look. Their reception was—"

"Outside at the ranch. I see the problem. But Angie's reception is at the Buffalo."

"I dunno. It's really a bright red."

"And the Buffalo is chock-a-block with red Valentine stuff. You'll blend right in."

"I guess it is. I hadn't figured out what I'd wear."

"Then wear this. For me."

Her breath hitched. He was in deep. And so was she.

13

As soon as the words came out of his mouth, Lucky regretted saying them. He and Oksana had agreed to the terms of this arrangement. It ended tomorrow.

Yet he'd just asked her to wear the red dress on Wednesday for Dallas and Angie's wedding. Worse yet, he'd asked her to wear it for him.

Her tender expression told him she'd registered that request as exactly what it was, a plea from a besotted cowboy. "Sorry." He shoved his fingers through his hair. "I shouldn't have—"

"Don't be tough on yourself. I'm the one who got us into this. If anybody should apologize, it's me. If I wear that dress to the wedding, you know damn well I'll be wearing it for you. Who else would I wear it for?"

He knew the answer to that one. "Yourself. It's your Sigourney Weaver dress. The one that makes you feel strong."

"It's the funniest thing." She gazed at him, her dark eyes filled with warmth. "Ever since I moved to Wagon Train, I haven't felt the need to pump myself up by wearing it."

"That's good to hear. Then I take back what I said. If you don't need it for you, it can stay in the closet." He put it back where he'd found it.

"We'll see. I don't have to decide now. Gonna fetch my Ugg boots?"

"Yes, ma'am." Leaning over, he picked them up in one hand and used the other to grab his boots from where he'd kicked them off earlier. He carried both over to the sitting area.

"This town feels like a safe haven." She took the red chair to pull on her boots and he took the shabby one. "I'll have to ask Ella if bullying is a problem here the way it is in other places."

"I doubt it. We look out for one another, and that goes for all ages and circumstances."

"Like the family who had the fire right before Christmas?"

"Like that." He shoved his feet into his well-worn boots. It was time he told her this. "A little closer to home, there's my birth mother."

"Oh?"

"She didn't know a soul or have a penny to her name, but the hotel let her stay and the hospital accepted her into the maternity ward when her time came. Without the kindness shown her, I might not be alive." He glanced up, prepared to see pity in her eyes. Instead she watched him with interest. "Don't know why I brought that up."

"Because you trust me?"

His breath caught. The air between them crackled with awareness as he met her gaze. "Yes. And I hadn't figured out how much until right now. You inspire trust, Oksana. You'll make a hell of a counselor."

She blushed. "Thank you." She hesitated. "Will you tell me her name?"

His chest tightened as it always did when he let himself consider the facts. "She gave it as Judy Smith. Which made it impossible to trace her after she died. That was probably her intention."

"She didn't want to be found."

"No." And he was afraid to know the reason in case it was something awful. "Mom said she had an Irish brogue you could cut with a skean."

"What's a skean?"

"An ancient Irish dagger. Mom's a treasure-trove of info like that."

"Then maybe your birth mother was born in Ireland."

"Could have been. My lowlife father might have been Irish, too, but no one in town remembers him. He came and went just that fast."

"Leaving her totally alone."

"And covered in shame because of it. Mom thinks it was partly what killed her." He sucked in a breath. Sometimes, in the middle of the night, he could feel that shame creeping over him.

"It's a powerful emotion."

"According to Mom, she'd expected my father to marry her. Instead he left her, nine months pregnant and no resources, in a room at the Wagon Train Hotel."

"Which means you have no way to trace him, either."

"That's about the size of it. A part of me wants to know something. Another part of me wonders if I'm better off not knowing." He scrubbed his cold hands over the soft denim covering his thighs. "It's not exactly an uplifting story. Thanks for listening."

"I'm honored that you told me."

"I felt you should know." Why did he have to go and say that? Except it was true. He didn't want her clinging to some sanitized version of who he was. Or did it matter? This was a one-night stand, after all.

"And I appreciate getting the details. Angie told me Desiree adopted you at the same time she had Rance, but she didn't elaborate. I halfway expected Rance to blurt out some tidbits when he was hanging around the bookstore, but he never did."

"He wouldn't. He acts like he doesn't have a filter, but when it comes to the big stuff, he absolutely does. That goes for the whole family. No one would have told you what I just did. It was up to me."

"And since you have..." She stood. "I want to tell you about what's in that box under the bed."

"The box under the bed!" He leaped up. "I can't believe I forgot about it. That was the first thing I meant to check on after I got dressed and put on some boots." He started over toward the collapsed bedframe.

"Wait. Before you start moving any of that, you need gloves. We both do."

"Good point. I'll fetch the ones from the storeroom."

"I'll start sweeping. By the way, did you bring that bedroll?"

He blinked. "What bedroll?"

"The one Gil told you to make up so you could sleep on the floor down there."

"Oh, *that* bedroll. Yes, I did."

"You might want to roll it out and toss the covers a bit, just in case anyone shows up in the morning to check on us."

"Do you think they will?" He glanced at the broken bed. "Because I can't get rid of the evidence that fast."

"Don't worry. Nobody comes up here. And they certainly wouldn't without asking. I can say my apartment's a total mess and I don't want anyone to see it."

He let out a breath. "You're right." Then he grinned. "Besides, nobody would believe I was responsible for that broken bed even if they saw it."

"Exactly. But they might believe I got stir-crazy and decided to use it as a trampoline."

"Uh-uh. I'm not letting you take the rap. But you won't have to because we're not letting anyone up here until I've carted the pieces off to the dump." He started toward the door. "Anything else you need from downstairs?"

"I don't think so."

"Then I'll be right back."

"Oh, hang on. Brownies. I took the container down to have some with my coffee this morning and left it there."

His taste buds perked up. Her home-baked brownies rocked. He'd been too busy thinking about her body to remember she'd baked some yesterday. "How many are left?"

"Enough to share with you, if that's what you're asking."

"I'll get 'em." He took the stairs at a good clip and cool air greeted him. The main floor thermostat automatically turned down the heat every night.

The glow of security lights allowed him to see as he shook out the hasty bedroll he'd made from the sheets and blankets in the Metalworks' back room. He'd brought a pillow, too, so he pounded a dent in the middle to simulate where his head had been.

How long would this stolen night remain a secret? If he and Oksana played it cool, maybe forever. That was a long damn time to not be holding her in his arms. But he was never meant to do that on a permanent basis, anyway.

He quickly ditched that unproductive thought and located the brownies on the shelf under the cash register. He could smell them even with the cover on the glass container.

Flipping on the light in the storeroom, he picked up the work gloves. He and Oksana used them when a carton of books arrived looking like it had been dragged over the tarmac. Who'd have guessed he'd need gloves to pick up pieces of a broken bedframe?

Normally he'd be wracked with guilt over a stunt like that. Not this time. When he'd climbed in, he'd had two goals — to give Oksana a great time and break that cheesy bed.

Why had that second goal appealed to him so much? Because it sure had. Somehow it was tied to the red chair, but he couldn't figure out the connection. Maybe he was just sick of putting up with inferior stuff.

Except he wasn't the one who'd had to. She hadn't minded the chair or the bed. Clearly they'd bothered the hell out of him, though.

Brownies and gloves in hand, he took the stairs two at a time, eager to get back to her. Now he could admit that every afternoon he'd forced himself to leave the shop and return to his beautiful log cabin. He still couldn't believe it was his.

But a part of him had yearned to stay after the store closed and climb these stairs. He'd fooled himself into thinking it was the apartment that called to him, the experience of being steps away from all those books.

That had figured in, but she'd been the draw. And here he was, living the dream. For one night. Which was as it should be.

She'd just emptied the contents of the dustpan into the trash when he walked through the door. Her smile of welcome generated heat in his chest that soon traveled elsewhere. He wanted her again. But they had work to do.

"I see you found the brownies. That can be our treat after we get the bedroom area livable."

"I'm on board with that." He had a different treat in mind and the brownies could wait as far as he was concerned. But no point in mentioning it until they'd finished their chores.

He set the container on the kitchen counter and handed over her pair of gloves. "Let the record show that I want to kiss you and I'm not going to."

"Let the record show that I felt like grabbing you when you came through the door, but I didn't."

"Where were you planning to grab me?"

"Whatever part I could easily get hold of." She glanced down at his fly. "When you arrived, that was a promising area."

"It seems I missed you."

"Missed you, too." She leaned the broom handle against the counter and set the dustpan on the floor next to it. "I pulled the bedding off and left it on the red chair."

"Saw that." He put on his gloves and walked over to the dismantled bed. "If we carry the mattress and box springs to the sitting area we can pile the remains of the bed against the wall and move the two chairs and the lamp over where the bed was."

"And we can make love in front of the fire."

"Yes, ma'am." Slow, sweet love, the polar opposite of breaking-the-bed love.

"Okay, let's do it." She pulled on her gloves.

They finished in under fifteen minutes. He wasn't surprised. They'd always worked well together, even on the first day, sometimes talking, sometimes silent, but unerringly picking up each other's unspoken rhythm.

After they remade the bed, they dimmed the lights. Perched on the mattress facing the cast-iron stove, they munched on brownies from the container between them.

They'd both ditched their boots and the crushed file box of Oksana's stuff sat by her bare feet. The box was half its original height. But since it had been only half-full, the contents were basically okay.

Oksana pulled out several spiral-bound notebooks and set them on the floor beside the box. "The yellow one is for solid, workable ideas. The red one is for memories, both good and bad. The blue one is for crazy, far-out concepts. The green one is for developing ideas from the yellow one."

He nodded as if he had a clue where this was going. Then she picked up what looked like a bound manuscript about an inch thick, the sort of thing his mom got from publishers wanting an endorsement for the author.

She plopped it into her lap. "This is my book."

"*Your* book?" He looked more closely at the cover page. *THE LIFE AND TIMES OF ODETTE BIDELSPACH by Oksana Jones.* "You wrote this?"

"I did. And I've started the next one. It's on my laptop. I wouldn't have a print copy of this one except my mother prefers to read print. She was my first and only reader."

"When did you do this? When did you have *time* to do this?"

"At night when I was tired of studying. Or in the early morning when I'd wake up with the characters talking in my head. It's a series about a very tall girl who has a funny name. Bet you wonder where I got that idea."

"You wrote a book. In your spare time." He was having trouble processing the information. "How long did it take to—"

"I started it when I came on board here. I've had the idea for ages, but selling other people's books galvanized me. I'm writing it for girls going through what I went through so they don't feel so alone."

"I'm bowled over. I don't know what I expected, but it wasn't this. You're a writer. How could you not tell me?"

"Because I'm not telling anyone. Just my mom. And now you. I want to get at least two books done, maybe three, before I try to get it published."

"Will you let me read it?"

"Would you want to? You're not a—"

"A girl? What difference does it make? I'm a reader. I manage a bookstore. I read everything. You know that."

"I thought you did it so you could talk to any customer who comes in."

"That's one reason, but I also do it because good writing is good writing, no matter what the subject is."

"I can't tell if this is good writing, but I don't think it's bad writing. My mother loved it, of course. If I let you read it, promise you'll tell me the truth."

"I promise." He had a gut feeling it would be great.

"If you think it's publishable, my next step is to seek out a published writer for advice. I don't know any."

She knew a *New York Times* bestselling author. She just didn't realize it.

"That's one of the reasons I've been trying to get a response from M.R. Morrison."

Oh, boy. He had to talk to his mom. Except that was territory filled with land mines. He might be able to hide his feelings about Oksana from his sister and brothers. But his mom? No way.

14

Oksana's stomach churned a little as she handed her book to Lucky. This must be how a mother felt when surrendering her child to a babysitter for the first time.

As a first reader, her mom had been a safe bet. But this guy had devoured a ton of great books, from classics to recent *New York Times* bestsellers. Although he would be kind no matter what he thought, she didn't want kindness. She wanted him to love it.

"You look a little scared."

"Because I am."

His voice gentled. "I don't have to read it. Want it back?"

Tempting. She could always give it to him later. Maybe she should wait until she'd finished book two. Or better yet, after the third was done.

"I know I asked, but that's a knee-jerk reaction. It's your first book." He held it out. "Keep it to yourself as long as you need to."

She took a deep breath. "I want you to read it. If I follow through with this, complete strangers will be reading what I write."

"Yes, they will."

"Besides, I need feedback other than my mother's biased praise. I want your honest opinion. That's scary because your opinion matters so much, but..." She gazed at him. "I have to get used to being scared."

"Yes, ma'am. Putting a book out into the world is like standing in Times Square naked. Or so I've heard."

"I believe it. I read every author interview I can find and they talk about that vulnerability. Writing and publishing isn't for the faint of heart."

"Good thing you have the heart of a lion, then."

"Me?"

"Yes, you." He laid the book carefully on the floor next to the bed. "The kids at school didn't break you and neither did the idiot who derailed your education. And now you've written a book. Do you know how many people in the world can say that?"

"No."

"Less than one percent."

"Wow. Where did you hear that?"

"From my mom. Like I said, she's a treasure-trove of interesting info."

"And obviously she's a bookworm like you since she decided to open this shop. I've never asked, but I assume this is your dream job."

He hesitated. Then he looked away and focused on the dancing flames of the cast-iron stove. "It is, and selling books is all I've ever wanted to do, and still is, but...."

She waited. If he let it drop, she would, too.

Then he turned back to her. "Lately I've been feeling restless. Managing the shop was a thrill when I was younger. I was proud of doing it. But it's not enough anymore. I need a bigger challenge."

"Like what?" The news didn't surprise her.

"Expanding, opening L'Amour and More bookshops in other small towns that don't have one. Apple Grove doesn't."

"The place where the cider comes from?"

"Yep. It's also where Mom grew up. She went back with Sky and Beau two years ago. When they came back she tossed out the idea of opening one. But she hasn't brought it up again."

"That might have something to do with grandchildren coming on the scene."

"No doubt. Babies are her jam. But I've been thinking about it since then, especially recently. Beau says it's a lot like Wagon Train, a friendly little town that expands every summer when tourists arrive."

"Which means L'Amour and More might fit right in."

"And what if it did?" Excitement flared in his eyes. "We'd model it on this one — same size, same personal service, good coffee and snacks, reading nooks. And thanks to your brilliant suggestion last summer, complimentary Bluetooth headsets if customers want country tunes while browsing."

"Would you be managing both?"

"I'd have to at first, until we know it's solid." His voice grew more animated. "A rental space with an option to buy would be perfect, so we can ease into it. But first I'd hire Trent to research the customer base. I just found out that's his job— market analyst."

"Aha. So that's why he can live anywhere. I wondered."

"I didn't know it before, either. I was stoked when he told us on the way back from Missoula. I want data before diving in. I can't ignore the popularity of digital books, but my instincts tell me folks still like cozy bookshops and physical copies to hold."

"They certainly do in this town." She'd never heard him talk like this. His confidence was sexy. Her fingers tingled with the urge to touch him, but she held back. She didn't want to derail him when he was so into his subject. "Twenty-plus years of profitability is a good track record."

"It'll look good to the Wagon Train Bank when I go in and ask for a business loan."

That surprised her. "You'd secure the financing yourself?"

"That's my plan. I'll need Mom to agree I can use the name, but I want to finance it myself. I'd use my house as collateral. That way if I fail, I'll be the only one affected."

"I'll take a wild guess you haven't talked to her about any of this."

He shook his head. "There's always something, either a baby due or a wedding on the horizon. I've had trouble finding the right time."

"Have you told anyone your ideas?"

"Just you."

"Sounds like you need to start spreading the news."

He gazed at her, his smile eager, his eyes sparkling. "You could be right."

"I am right. I haven't seen you this excited since you found that signed copy of *Rivers West.*"

"Oh, I think you have." He put the brownie container on top of the cast-iron stove and pulled her close. "Unless you haven't been paying attention."

Close contact set her on fire. She snuggled against him and wound her arms around his neck. "I wasn't talking about sex."

"Well, I'm talking about it." He nibbled on her lips. "Care to join the discussion?"

"Love to. But there's a little matter of—"

"Under my pillow." He tipped his head toward the one closest to the cast-iron stove.

Her pulse raced. "Thinking ahead, were you?"

"Always. Are we good to go?"

"I soon will be." Wiggling out of his arms, she rolled to the far side of the bed. "Can't speak for you." She sat up and stripped off her top.

He yanked off his T-shirt. "No fair. You have on less than I do."

"Want some help?" She tossed her bottoms on the floor.

"I've got it." Standing, he unfastened his jeans, shoved them down and stepped away.

She gulped. "I would agree." The view from this angle was awe-inspiring.

Kneeling on the mattress, he held her gaze as he retrieved the condom, ripped open the package and sheathed his impressive equipment. "Not gonna get under the covers?"

"I'm counting on you to keep me warm."

"Job accepted." Moving over her, he settled in. His body lightly touched hers, surrounding her with heat without giving her his weight... or making the ultimate connection. "How's that?"

"Nice." She slipped her arms around his neck. She'd dreamed that someday a man would look at her the way Lucky was looking at her now.

The depth of emotion in his eyes told her they'd shot way past mere physical gratification. Now they were truly making love.

"I don't want to rush."

"Me, either."

"I want time to do this." He threaded his fingers through her hair as it lay on the pillow. Slowly he let it slide free. "I knew your hair would feel like silk."

"You've thought about it?"

"I didn't think so... but I must have."

Reaching up, she stroked his beard. "When you grew this, I got goosebumps every time I was close enough to touch you."

Catching her hand, he kissed the tips of her fingers. "You should have seen your face when I threatened to shave it off."

"And you didn't figure out I was nutty about you?"

"I wouldn't let myself know it." Dipping his head, he kissed her lips, her cheeks, her nose, her forehead. "Just like you."

The light touch of his mouth left her trembling.

"You're shivering." He nuzzled the side of her neck. "And I promised to keep you warm. Are you cold?"

"Not even close." She ran her fingers over his broad shoulders and traced the line of his collarbone, making him shudder. "Cold?"

"Not even close." He lifted his head, his green eyes dark as a forest at twilight. "I ache for you, Oksana."

"I'm here."

"Which makes me a very blessed man." He eased forward gently, almost reverently, as if savoring the journey.

She welcomed him with a rush of moisture and a low moan of pleasure. She'd live for this moment, and the next and the next, until she ran out of moments with this incredible man.

If there was a price to pay, and there always was, Lucky McLintock was worth it.

_15_

This would be the last time. Although Oksana would never admit she was tired, Lucky had learned to recognize the signs — a flutter of her dark lashes, a swallowed yawn, a muffled sigh.

He should be tired, too. Nope. He had one more chance to taste the sweetest lovemaking he'd ever known and he would give it his all. He could look at this stolen night as a cruel joke or a gift. He chose the latter.

Thrusting slowly, he held her gaze. She'd cradled him with her body, sliding her arms around his back and hooking her legs over his thighs.

He rocked in her embrace, soaking up the light shining in her eyes and giving it right back. The flames from the cast-iron stove glowed on her skin and played peekaboo in her glossy hair.

He never wanted this moment to end, but it was already slipping away. Her small gasp signaled time was up. Then her grip tightened. He reluctantly answered her unspoken plea and stroked faster.

His climax shouldered its way forward, too. He wouldn't fight it, wouldn't push for more. She needed sleep.

She murmured his name. The soft way she said it got to him, almost made him respond with something he shouldn't. Not now. Not ever.

The first wave of her orgasm rolled over his cock. "Lucky." Louder this time. "Come with me."

"I will." He pumped faster, giving them both what they needed.

When she cried out and lifted her hips, he sank deep and let the whirlwind take him. Swallowing the words that rose to his lips, he rested his forehead on her shoulder. If he looked into her beautiful eyes, he might blurt it out.

Her breathing slowed. "That was lovely."

"Yes, ma'am." His voice was a little rough around the edges. Better not linger. He was still dangerously close to telling her. "I won't be long." He left the bed.

"'kay."

He'd told a little white lie. He took his time cleaning up while he fought the urge to spill his guts. He was desperate to say those words, more eager than he'd been to break the bed.

But a man had hijacked her dreams once before. She'd been in love with that dude. He'd bet on it. And she was in love with him, for some crazy reason. Poor choice on her part.

She'd get over it, especially if he didn't tell her how he felt. He didn't return to her until he'd won the battle and could guarantee he'd keep his mouth shut.

She lay facing his side of the bed, her arm across his pillow, as if she expected him to return and rest his head there. Her dark lashes lay against her cheek and her breasts rose and fell in an easy, relaxed rhythm.

Maybe she was playing possum. Crouching down, he murmured her name. She didn't stir.

If he climbed in next to her, she might wake up. And he had no wish to sleep. He picked up his clothes and *THE LIFE AND TIMES OF ODETTE BIDELSPACH.*

He justified choosing the red chair because the light was slightly brighter in that part of the room. He laid the manuscript on it while he dressed and fetched the ottoman.

Then he picked up Oksana's book and lowered his butt into the chair. He'd never sat in it, figuring it didn't matter whether he liked it.

Turned out he did. After he propped his bare feet on the ottoman and leaned back, he wished he'd bought a second one for himself. Evidently his added height didn't alter the physics of the situation. It was still a damned good chair.

With a smile of anticipation, he opened the manuscript and began to read.

He didn't move from that spot until his phone chimed. Rance. Leaping up, he set the manuscript on the ottoman, hurried to the kitchen and snatched his phone from the counter.

He glanced over at the bed as he put the phone to his ear with a muttered *what.* Oksana was sitting up looking around as if trying to orient herself.

Rance sounded bouncy as a puppy with a new toy. "Coming to your rescue, bro! Mrs. J told me you were at the shop, but when I got no answer I called Gil who told me you're stuck with a bedroll on the floor. I can only imagine how miserable you must be with that setup. Me and Midnight Thunder are comin' to getcha."

"Thanks, but if you can drive in, I can drive out."

"That's not what Mrs. J said. That ol' blizzard dumped twice as much snow on the town as it did out here."

"Is that right?" He switched his phone to speaker mode so Oksana could hear. "Twice as much?"

"That's the word. Good thing it's Sunday and most things are normally closed. The Buffalo won't be opening today, that's for sure. Your truck's likely buried like every other vehicle that's not in a garage. It'll be tomorrow before they get that mess cleaned up."

"If that's the case, how can you get to me?"

"Mom's letting me hook up the blade to Thunder. I'll plow my way in. And out."

"I see." No wonder his brother was excited. He'd been dying to test his fancy F-350 on some massive job. Plowing into town would suit him just fine.

"So pack up that bedroll and thank Oksana for feeding you, 'cause I know she did. Bet she gave you some of those brownies she makes."

"Yep." And she was looking straight at him, her glorious hair tousled and the covers wrapped around her shoulders because the frigid air outside had a way of seeping in, especially on the second floor.

"I'm leaving in a few minutes, so I should be there in about forty-five. Does Oksana need me to bring her anything? Mrs. J said she's fine, but if Oksana's low on something, I can bring her supplies."

"I'll ask." And he would have, right this minute, if she hadn't made a slashing motion across her throat. "Hang on. I'll go upstairs and tap on her door. She might still be asleep."

"Could since it's Sunday. I knew you wouldn't be. It's after seven."

"It is?" He checked the time on his phone. Sure enough. Ducking out the door with his phone, he tromped down a few stairs and back up. Then he rapped on the open door. "Oksana? You up?"

Wrapped in a blanket, she walked over. Although she was smiling, sadness dimmed the light in her eyes. "I am, now."

"Sorry to wake you. Seems that the town is snowed in and Rance is using a plow to come fetch me. He wants to know if you need anything."

She mouthed the word *you*, which got him right in the gut.

Then she spoke up. "Thanks, Rance. I'm all set. Take care driving in."

"You know I will. Got an extra brownie for me as a reward?"

"Sure thing."

"See you both soon." He disconnected.

"Damn." Lucky groaned as he tapped the screen to close the connection. "I thought we'd have more time."

"So did I. And we'd better get moving. Or I should, anyway. I need a shower and some coffee. I have to be dressed and down there looking perky when he arrives. You, however, can—" Then she stared at him. "Why do you have your clothes on?"

"When I came back to bed, you were asleep. I didn't feel tired, so I got dressed and started reading your book."

"And dozed off?"

"No, ma'am. I was reading when he called."

"You read all *night*?"

He shrugged. "I got into the story, and your red chair is comfy."

"How much did you read?" Without waiting for an answer, she scurried over to the chair, trailing the blanket behind her, and picked up the manuscript.

He followed her. "I'm about two thirds in. She's dealing with her first period. You did a great job with that. Angie would love it. She—"

"I can't believe you sat for hours reading my book." After flipping through to find the part he'd mentioned, she glanced over the page. Then she closed the book and laid it gently on the ottoman. "That blows me away."

"If Rance hadn't called, I'd still be reading it. I've never been an eleven-year-old girl, but I have a pretty good idea what that's like after living in Odette's head for a few hours. She's a great character. She's smart, and funny, and—" He broke off as Oksana grabbed his face in both hands.

Then she kissed him on the mouth, hard, but not nearly long enough. She pulled back, her eyes sparkling. "Thank you, thank you, a million times, thank you! I can tell you're not just saying that."

"I hope so, because I mean every word. You're an excellent writer. This can't be the first thing you've ever done."

"It's not. I've been scribbling poems and stories since first grade, but then basketball came along and I... anyway, this is the first thing I've done in a while."

"It needs to be published."

"I don't know how."

"I'll see what I can do to help you with that."

"A small press would be fine. Or maybe I could put it online myself. I don't care about the money. It will be a side gig, anyway."

"Don't be too sure. You've written something that will appeal to both kids and adults."

"That's nice to hear, but the last time I tried doing what I love to make money it was a disaster. I really, really appreciate you taking all that time and the wonderful things you said, though." She kissed him again. "I need a shower." Tossing away the blanket, she made tracks for the bathroom.

He watched her walk away, his chest tight with anxiety. If he wasn't careful, she was liable to put him in the same category as the loser who had convinced her she could be a basketball star in Europe and rake in the dough.

Except that guy was a fraud who'd bragged about connections that didn't bring her the riches he'd promised. That wasn't the case here. As a

McLintock, even an adopted McLintock, he had the mother of all connections, literally.

That said, writing wasn't a job with a steady paycheck. As he'd seen first-hand, it was a financial rollercoaster. Oksana's plan to become a school counselor was more likely to give her a stable income.

A counselor's job would allow her to help hundreds of kids. But if she became a bestselling author, she could reach thousands. And she could live anywhere, like in Wagon Train, for example.

And maybe someday....

Aw, hell, who did he think he was, having ideas like that? He could forget that one. Oksana would always be out of reach.

_16_

Oksana moved quickly through her showering routine. She used a scrunchy to create a high ponytail so her hair wouldn't get wet. Then she soaped up fast and rinsed just as fast. She couldn't let anything slow her down, least of all Lucky's thrilling reaction to her book.

But no matter how hard she worked to stuff that conversation into a small corner of her brain, it ran on a loop as she showered. His praise had surpassed her wildest dreams. Sitting for hours engrossed in her words demonstrated that he wasn't making it up.

He could easily get lost in a book. She'd witnessed it. By staying up all night reading Odette's story, he'd given her the ultimate compliment and the confidence to see this project through.

She wouldn't get carried away, though. Not this time. She'd been naïve about the opportunities, or lack of them, in basketball. But everyone knew that freelance writers struggled to make a living.

If less than one percent of the world's population wrote a complete book, how tiny was the percentage of writers who found people willing to buy it?

Also, Lucky adored her and so naturally he'd adore Odette, a character who shared many of her characteristics. No wonder he pictured the book sweeping the bestseller lists.

Her mother had said the same sort of thing after finishing it. So far two people had commented on her work and they both loved her to pieces. She still didn't have an unbiased opinion, and until she got one, she'd be wise not to get too full of herself.

She came out of the steamy bathroom wrapped in a towel, more for the warmth than for modesty. The scent of brewed coffee greeted her.

Lucky wasn't in the apartment, but he'd been busy. All the pieces of the bed except the headboard were gone. Where the heck had he stashed them?

She'd put on her underwear by the time he bounded up the stairs and through the door, fully dressed and wearing work gloves. "Thanks for making coffee." She took a long-sleeved T-shirt out of the drawer.

"You're welcome." His gaze warmed. "Nice outfit."

She cherished the moment, the quiver deep in her body generated by the heat in his eyes. His beard wasn't as neat this morning, giving him a slightly rougher look. She wanted to strip off his clothes and push him down on the unmade bed.

But Rance was on his way, so she pulled the T-shirt over her head to hide the flush rising to her cheeks. "What did you do with the siderails and slats?"

"They're in the storeroom, leaning upright in a corner." He swallowed and glanced away, as if he might be struggling with the same urges she was. "I hated leaving you with all that junk piled up against the wall. I made a place to stash the headboard, too. You can put the furniture back the way you had it."

"Is there enough space in the storeroom? We need to be able to move around in there." She sat in her chair to put on socks before taking a clean pair of jeans from the closet. She avoided his gaze, reasonably sure he was watching her every move and wishing his brother hadn't called.

"It'll be okay. It's temporary." He sighed. "Damn, Oksana. I don't want to leave."

"I don't want you to, either." She zipped up her jeans. "But you don't have a choice."

"You're right. If I'd told him I was fine with a bedroll on the floor he wouldn't have believed me."

"Why not? Isn't that a cowboy thing?" She picked up her leather boots from the closet floor.

"It's supposed to be, but I've never liked that, even when we were kids. The whole family knows it. I was the one who complained about sleeping on the ground when we went camping."

"Did you try an air mattress?" Tugging on her boots, she got to her feet.

"Still didn't like it. I want a sturdy bed and a cushy mattress."

"I'm getting that." She glanced at him. Oh, yeah, he was thinking the same hot thoughts she was about beds and mattresses. He needed to take that headboard and get out of here, but she was standing in the way.

"I could use some of that coffee you made." She hurried past him. "Want a cup?"

"Maybe after I take this downstairs." He crossed to the headboard and turned it on its side.

"Now that I know that about you, I'm surprised you didn't replace the bedframe while you were living here." She poured a mugful of coffee.

"Believe me, I wanted to." Picking up the headboard, he carried it to the doorway and set it down as he gauged the opening. "But I was socking money away for my cabin."

"I'll bet your mom—"

"Probably, but she'd given me a job, after all." He glanced at her. "And my life, if you get right down to it. She also gave me the McLintock name. That's more than enough for a kid who came into the world with nothing."

A kid who came into the world with nothing. Was that how he pictured himself? Sounded like it.

"At least this sorry excuse for a bed frame is history, and you'll have a new one this week. You won't have to keep the mattress and box spring on the floor for long.

"No rush. You have Angie's wedding."

"I know, but the weather's predicted to do a one-eighty. The snow should start melting tomorrow. By Tuesday I should be able to get rid of the remains and pick up a new bed from Missoula at the end of the week."

"Okay. You're the boss." Time to remind herself of that now that the fun and games had ended.

He frowned. "I didn't mean to make it sound as if I'd buy one without consulting you."

"Why not? I'm only renting. Whatever you find will be better than what was here."

"I want to get something you like, though. We'll talk about it. I'll be back in a few minutes." He picked up the headboard, maneuvered it out the door and carried it down the stairs.

What was he thinking? A discussion of bedframes was the last thing they needed, especially in the apartment where they'd been making love only hours ago. Maybe her responsible, considerate, gorgeous boss hadn't thought that through.

Carrying her coffee to the bathroom, she brushed her hair and put it into a regular ponytail. She didn't bother with makeup. Rance wouldn't expect that since they'd have no customers today.

She'd been dreading his arrival but not anymore. Lucky couldn't very well discuss bedframe replacement once Rance arrived. How much longer before he was due? When he'd called he'd mentioned it was after seven, but how much after seven?

Walking out of the bathroom, she checked her phone sitting on the top of the dresser. Almost eight. Rance would be here soon, but not soon enough. Lucky was coming up the stairs, eager to talk about beds.

She refreshed her coffee, picked up the container of brownies and walked out the door. "I'm heading downstairs. I left the coffeepot on, so would you please turn it off after you pour yourself some?"

He blinked. "Um, sure. Makes sense to wait in the shop."

"That's what I thought." She moved aside so he could pass her on the landing. "See you down there."

Lucky hadn't turned on the overheads in the shop and if the sun was out, its light hadn't managed to penetrate the frosted-over windows. She set the brownies and coffee on the cash wrap next to where he'd left his coat. Then she threw the main switch for the overheads. The brighter the better.

"I didn't think you'd want those on today." Lucky came down the stairs with his mug of coffee.

"It's temporary, so it's not so gloomy down here. I'll turn them off after you guys leave."

He grimaced and set his mug on the cash wrap. "Leave 'em on all day if that helps."

"I shouldn't have used the word *gloomy*. It's not really—"

"It's the perfect word. I'm abandoning you when you're snowed in. That just seems wrong."

"It's actually the best scenario. We'll have a nice break from each other, which'll give us a chance to recalibrate and put what's happened in perspective."

"Yeah, but I'll have my family to distract me. You'll be forced to handle it by yourself. You can't hop over to the Buffalo if you feel the need for some company."

Damn. She should have known he'd feel guilty leaving. "I wouldn't if I could. I have classwork and my second book is calling to me. I'll be too busy to wallow. If you're picturing me turning into a soggy mess after you're gone, it won't be happening. "

"I know, but—" A deep rumble followed by the distinctive blare of a Ford truck horn ended the conversation. Grabbing his coat, he shoved his arms into the sleeves. "That'll be Rance. I'd better go see if I can get the door open."

"I didn't think of that. Snow's liable to be piled against it."

"Rance won't let that stop him, but it would be nice if he doesn't have to dig us out. He might decide to use the blade. I don't want him nicking the door." Unlocking it, he gave a tug. When the door remained closed, he braced himself and used both hands.

With a sharp crack, the door popped open and he staggered back. Waist-high snow kept him from stepping outside. It also kept Rance from continuing his plan. The large black truck jerked as he slammed on the brakes. Clearly he'd intended to remove the snow with the imposing blade attached to the front of it.

Frigid air swept into the store as Lucky yelled at him. Something about shovels. Then he backed up a few steps. "Get yours and I'll get mine!"

Closing the door, he strode in her direction, laying his phone on the cash wrap as he passed by. "Maybe he wouldn't have damaged it, but I'm not taking any chances. It's at least seventy-five years old, maybe older, and solid as a rock. But that doesn't mean it can stand up to a blade with three-hundred and fifty horsepower behind it."

"So you're gonna dig a path out to him?"

"I'll dig from this side. He tossed a shovel in his truck before he left, so he can dig from the street side." He paused to glance over his shoulder at her. "It won't take us long, but maybe you should go upstairs and close your door so you don't freeze. I'll need to leave this one open for a little bit."

"I'll just get my coat. I'm not missing the show."

He laughed. "You're easily entertained."

"So I've been told." Watching him use his impressive muscles to conquer the snow sure beat the multiple-choice exam she had waiting on her laptop.

By the time she came downstairs wearing what he called her Red Riding Hood parka, he'd removed enough that he was standing on the doorsill. He kept up a steady rhythm, his breath clouding the air as he sent shovelfuls flying to his right, piling more on the existing snowbank.

To his left, his truck looked like a ghost vehicle mired up to the door handle in snow and crusted over with ice. Clouds still blocked the sun, but the blizzard was over.

Positioned in front of the grill of his truck, Rance mirrored Lucky's actions. Then he paused to catch his breath and spotted her standing inside the doorway. "Hey, Oksana! Mom told me to convince you to come stay at her place today and tonight. She doesn't want to leave you stranded here by yourself."

Lucky paused abruptly, obviously waiting for her answer.

For a second she considered it. Angie had given her a tour of the house during Ella and Marsh's wedding reception. No doubt there would be a crackling fire going all day and meals that she didn't have to cook, although she'd happily pitch in. The library was to die for.

But she needed to separate herself from Lucky and the McLintock clan, not create a deeper bond. "Please tell her thanks," she called out. "That's extremely kind, but I have coursework to catch up on."

Lucky's shovel went back into action.

"She figured you did." Rance kept shoveling, too. "You could bring your laptop and use either the library or set up by the fire. No one will bug you and she has great Wi-Fi."

That wasn't surprising. According to the rumors, Desiree McLintock was the wealthiest person in Wagon Train.

Spending the night in her lovely home would be a treat, an opportunity that might never come again. Maybe Lucky wouldn't even be there. After all, he had his own cabin.

That last part was pure rationalization. He'd be there, at least for dinner. Otherwise it would look as if he wanted to avoid her. Forced proximity would be tough on both of them. She had to turn down the invitation.

"It's a great offer, but I—" Before she could finish, the shop went dark.

"That settles it," Rance said cheerfully. "Your power's out. Now you have to come back with us."

<u>17</u>

"Maybe it just tripped a breaker." Lucky jammed his shovel into the snow. "Hey, bro, you should be able to see the neon sign in the barber shop from where you are. Is it on?"

"Sure is. Must just be you."

"Keep shoveling, then. I'll check the breaker box." He turned to face Oksana, who wore a *what now?* expression.

"I can check it for you," she said quickly.

He lowered his voice. "I know you can. Just come on back with me." He closed the door, eliminating what little light had come through it. Ice covering the bay window in front turned the shop into a dark cave. He turned on his flashlight app as he walked toward the storeroom "I don't want you to feel pressured by Rance."

"I'm not. He's just being sweet."

"I can tell you don't want to go out there." Because of him, and it broke his heart because she'd have a great time.

"Under different circumstances I'd love to. Just not today."

"I understand. I'm sure it's a breaker. Temps like this put an extra load on the system."

"And I'm the genius who threw the main switch a while ago."

"No problem. It's easily handled." He opened the metal box and shined the flashlight on it. "Huh." He studied it some more. "Nothing's been tripped."

"Then it's something else."

"Likely a power line issue. I'll notify them, but I doubt it'll get fixed tonight. That means shutting down the whole works." He flipped the main circuit breaker before pointing the flashlight at the floor, which gave him enough of a glow to gauge her reaction. "You'll have to come back to the ranch, after all. Sorry about that."

"It'll be fine." She met his gaze. "But I'm beginning to think Mother Nature is messing with us."

"Kinda feels that way." He hesitated. "This is going to sound off the wall, but as long as you're coming out there, how about bringing your book so Mom can read it?"

She frowned in puzzlement. "Why?"

He chose his words carefully. "Having the Wenches book club all these years has made her a decent judge of whether a book works or not. I admit I could be biased. Your mother certainly is. But Mom wouldn't be. And she'd keep it under wraps."

"Hey, you two, I finished the shoveling!" Rance's booted feet thumped on the floor. "I notice you're still in the dark. What's the deal, bro?"

"It's not the breaker," he called out. "It's something we can't fix right now, so Oksana's coming with us." He leaned close to her and kept his voice down. "Think about it."

She didn't answer.

Well, he'd made his pitch. Ever since his interrupted reading session, he'd wracked his brain looking for a way to get that story into his mother's hands without making a big deal of it or revealing her identity. Oksana wasn't ready for the world or even his family to know about her book. His mom would understand that immediately and tell no one.

This setup was perfect. Oksana could arrive with her laptop and whatever else she needed for her classes. The manuscript could be tucked in with her stuff where it would draw zero attention. Would she do it? He had no idea.

"Then let's get on the road." Rance met them as they left the storeroom.

Oksana quietly shut the door, although darkness hid the remains of the bed he'd stacked in there.

Good thing the power hadn't suddenly come on when it was open. The headboard was visible to anyone who looked inside and Rance would have recognized it. He'd been in that apartment often enough back when Lucky had lived there.

"I'll gather my things." Oksana started toward the darkened staircase.

"Better use the flashlight on your phone."

"It's upstairs."

"Then take mine." He handed it over, leaving him standing with Rance. The faint light coming through the frosted-over window panes didn't reach the cash wrap. "Got your phone?"

"Left it in the truck."

"Then I guess we'll just stand here in the dark until she gets back."

"I smell brownies."

"They're right beside you. If you can find them and take off the lid without knocking them on the floor, go ahead and have one. She'd want you to."

"Then I believe I will." He gently patted the cash wrap counter. "Aha! Got 'em."

The lid popped and the memory-laden fragrance of brownies poured out. He'd never eat them again without thinking about sitting on the bed with Oksana, the container between them, the promise of making love to her a sweet ache.

"I'm not positive but there might be three in there," Rance said. "Want one?"

"Not after you've touched them all."

"I barely—"

"Never mind. Take two. You did most of the shoveling."

"Nice of you to notice." His words were muffled by a chunk of brownie.

"I suppose you think I'm paranoid about the door."

"I would've stopped before I hit it."

"You sure about that?"

"Damn straight." He continued to talk with his mouth full. "My depth perception is legendary."

"And how many times have you operated that blade?"

"It happens to be my maiden voyage, but that doesn't mean—"

"It means you had at least a fifty-fifty chance of plowing into the door. But thank you for driving in."

"Good thing I did or you'd both be in a world of hurt. I had to come, though. I couldn't stand to think of you spending another night on the floor. You must have hated every minute."

"I managed." Thank God Rance couldn't see his face.

"Must've been worse than I thought. You sound a little choked up about it."

"It's over." There was a true statement that legitimately choked him up. He wouldn't dwell on it. "You know, two months ago Mom might not have invited Oksana to stay overnight."

"Then one of us would have offered Oksana a place to stay, probably you, since you know her the best."

"Yeah." He wouldn't dwell on that scenario, either.

"Well, I think it's great that Andy pushed for the renovation. Now he and Mom can toddle off to bed through a door like normal people. I get that she loves her revolving bookcase, but—"

"A door off the living room makes way more sense."

"And both their offices are still tucked out of sight. Most folks would never guess—"

"Cool it." The light from a phone bobbed as Oksana came down the stairs. He raised his voice. "I hope you left one for Oksana."

"Rance, did you find the brownies?"

"Yes, ma'am. Lucky told me to go ahead. I ate two. The last one's for you."

"You can have it. You deserve those brownies after driving in and then shoveling all that snow."

"Glad to be of service. Can I carry something for you?"

"I've got it, thanks. I just stuffed everything in a small duffel. It's light. Here's your phone, Lucky. Thanks." She handed it over.

His hand brushed hers as he took it back. Instant recall. He was back in bed with her, stroking—

"Then we're off," Rance said, his mouth full of the last brownie. "Got your bedroll, Lucky?"

"Bedroll. Right." Mussing up the covers and making a dent in the pillow had been a wasted effort. But where had he been when he'd done that?

Using his phone, he scanned the area around the cash wrap. Not there. In one of the aisles, then. Phone in hand, he started off.

"Where are you going, bro?"

"To find it."

"You can't remember where you slept?"

"I've repressed it."

Oksana snorted.

"Don't make fun of him," Rance murmured. "He's flexible about most everything, but he really, *really* hates a bad sleeping situation. I figure everyone has some little tic like that, so—"

"I can hear you." He almost tripped over the bedroll lying in the last aisle he checked.

Spooky. He'd laid it out next to the Young Adult section. "Found it."

"Great. Bro, you lead us out of here. You and your friend the bedroll can have the back seat. I'll take our guest around to the front."

She laughed. "You don't have to. I'm perfectly capable of getting in by myself."

"You're one of the most capable women I know, but this is your first ride in Midnight Thunder. You need to be handed in to commemorate the occasion."

"Oh, well, then. Who am I to buck tradition?"

Lucky's breath hitched. She would fit right in with his rambunctious family. After this sleepover, she'd be one of them. If she'd brought her book, she might become his mom's protégé.

Even when she left to take a job, she'd come back often. His heart would take a beating every time. Worse yet, hers might, too.

Had last night been worth it?

_18_

Oksana listened to Rance's stories about life on Rowdy Ranch and pretended her manuscript wasn't in the duffel at her feet. Just because she'd stuffed it in there at the last minute didn't mean she had to give it to Desiree. Lucky wouldn't say anything if she didn't.

He'd chosen to sit behind the driver's seat, so unless she looked out the side window, he was constantly in her peripheral vision. After notifying the electric company about the outage, he'd lounged against the leather upholstery and traded comments with his brother, smiling and laughing as if he didn't have a care in the world.

Doggone sexy guy was playing his part beautifully, and without sleep, too. Impressive. She might be more relaxed if she didn't have a manuscript that she might or might not show to the town's leading citizen, a woman who intimidated her a little, to be honest.

She could diffuse this ticking time bomb by deciding right now that she'd leave it in the duffel. But Lucky had made a good point about showing it to someone who would be more objective, someone who had plenty of practice evaluating books after running Wenches Who Read for years.

Oksana had never met a woman like her. Who has nine children and adopts a tenth without getting married? Then, after raising those kids by herself, she proposed to Andy Hartmann this past New Year's Eve. He hadn't fathered any of her children. Fascinating.

And where had her financial success come from? L'Amour and More couldn't have brought in enough to support that growing family.

A large inheritance? Unlikely. Receipts in the bookstore's files told of gradual renovations over the years. Ella had known the McLintocks since childhood and she remembered ongoing construction projects at the house, too.

Giving Desiree the book was a scary prospect, but it would have the advantage of bringing them closer. She might get a peek behind the curtain.

Maybe she'd discover nothing more exciting than a woman who'd learned how to play the stock market. But she had a hunch that wasn't the thing that motivated Desiree McLintock, the spark that made her want to get out of bed in the morning. If giving her the book would—

"So, Oksana, how d'ya like your new red chair?"

The question caught her completely off guard. Heat rose to her cheeks. "It's great!" She pasted a big ol' smile on her face and hoped Rance wouldn't notice he'd made her blush with that innocent question.

"Then it's comfortable? Because you should have seen my brother agonizing over the choice."

"I didn't *agonize.* I just wanted to make sure it was—"

"I don't know what you call it, then. Pacing around it, checking it from all angles. Turning it upside down to check the workmanship underneath. Asking the sales guy a million questions."

"I didn't want to saddle Oksana with something that wouldn't stand up."

"Obviously." Rance winked at her. "Trent thought he was buying it for his girlfriend."

She laughed and prayed it was convincing. "That's a riot. Too funny, right, boss?"

"Trent's never seen me buy furniture. That's just how I do it."

"That's certainly how you were when you bought the bed for your cabin," Rance said, "but you weren't nearly that picky when you went looking for other stuff."

"Yeah, I was. You didn't notice because you were too busy flirting with every sales lady we came across."

"There's some truth to that."

"Well, I appreciate all the trouble he took. It's a wonderful chair. I love it." She turned back to Lucky. "Thank you again for buying it."

"You're welcome." His steady gaze gradually warmed. "My pleasure."

Those green eyes sure could do a number on a gal. She swallowed and faced forward again. She'd have to limit how much time she spent looking at him for the next twenty-four hours. He was way too delicious.

Instead she surveyed the landscape as Rance drove down the frozen ranch road. "I see what you mean about the snow. The blizzard wasn't nearly as intense out here."

"Rowdy Ranch is like that, for some reason. Mom asked a meteorologist about it a few years ago. He had an explanation, but I don't remember it. Mom just says we're blessed."

"That I believe." She caught glimpses of log cabins through the trees as they passed unmarked sideroads. One of them could be Lucky's, but she didn't ask where his was located. Better not to know.

"You won't see Lucky's place," Rance said. "You have to go past Mom's before you get to his. Or mine, for that matter."

"Oh." Just as well.

"As soon as we were old enough, at least in Mom's estimation, she took me, Lucky and Angie on a drive around the ranch to choose a site for our cabins."

"She just assumed you'd be staying?"

"Why wouldn't she? We had the time of our lives on this ranch. We had horses to ride and acres to explore. It's a kid's version of paradise."

"It does seem ideal." Her parents would have loved to provide such surroundings for her and her brother. What had provided Desiree with the wherewithal to live like this? "Was it hard to choose?"

"Not for me. But Lucky — well, you tell her, bro."

He sighed. "Yeah, I took forever. She drove us all back home and then she and I went out again."

"They were gone for *hours*."

"I can't deny it. Looking back, I'm amazed that she didn't lose patience with me. But I finally found the perfect spot."

"What's it like?" She couldn't help herself.

"It's nestled in the trees. You can't even see the chimney from the road, let alone the roofline." He sounded proud of the fact.

"So it's hidden." That didn't surprise her.

"Yes, ma'am. And the building site is flat. They barely had to grade it. That cabin's solid as a rock. It's not going anywhere."

"That's a plus." Her heart swelled with empathy and love for the child in Lucky who desperately needed to know he stood on solid ground. He might have grown up in paradise, but he still wasn't sure he deserved it.

"And we're here." Rance took a road to the left, the only one with a modest wooden sign that read *Rowdy Ranch, D. McLintock.* It could be easily missed if a person didn't know to look for it. "Hey, bro, text Mom to let her know we brought Oksana."

"Will do."

The road curved gracefully to the right and ended in a wide space with the sprawling one-story house straight ahead and the outbuildings to the right and down a small slope. The snow dramatically changed the landscape, covering what used to be grassy areas dotted with wildflowers.

Trees surrounding the house had lost their leaves. Pale sunlight sparkled on what looked like icicles on the bare branches. But on closer inspection, she recognized the same fairy lights that had twinkled during the wedding reception in August. "Your mom leaves lights on the trees year-round?"

"She does," Lucky said. "At Christmas she doubles down. You could stand in the yard at midnight and read a book if you wanted."

She grinned and glanced back at him. "I have a hunch I'll have a great time today."

His gaze met hers. "I know you will." Pride shone in his eyes. "Mom just texted back. She's thrilled you're here."

The truth dawned on her. Deep down, he was proud of this place, and for a moment, he'd claimed his right to be a McLintock. Maybe she had a little something to do with that. What a lovely thought.

Rance pulled up next to a shoveled path leading to the front porch. "I'll let you two off here. Lucky, don't worry about the bedroll. I'll bring it in after I head down to the tractor barn and take off the blade."

"Need help with that, bro?"

"No, thanks." He took out his phone. "Either Sky or Buck should be around. I'm texting both of them now."

"Well, make sure, because—"

"I can ride down there, too, guys."

Rance flashed her a smile and held up his phone. "Sky's available, so we're covered. Lucky can take you on a tour later, after you've had something to eat. You probably missed breakfast."

"She did," Lucky opened his door and climbed out. "Oksana, let me come get you. It's not shoveled on your side."

"Oh, for pity's sake." Putting on her gloves, she opened her door. "I can—"

"Oksana." Rance laid a restraining hand on her arm. "Let my bonehead brother treat you like royalty. You're the best thing that's ever happened to that bookshop and I'm convinced he doesn't tell you that nearly enough."

"He's right, I don't." Lucky rounded the hood and came to her open door. "I intend to do better. First let me have your duffel." His breath fogged the air.

She lifted it off the floor and let him take it.

Hooking it over his shoulder, he held out his gloved hand. "I'll steady you as you get down. It's a little slippery."

Avoiding looking into those green eyes, she held onto him as she stepped into the snow. His firm grip sent urgent messages to every part of her body. Cold? Not her.

"Thanks, Rance." Lucky grabbed the door handle. "I owe you one, bro."

"Yes, yes, you do. You know I'll be collecting on that debt, too." He was still laughing as Lucky shut the door. Then he slowly pulled away.

Lucky still had a tight grip on her hand.

She looked over at him. "You can let go. I'm stable."

"I will, but I had to find out before we went in. Did you bring it?"

"Yes."

"Will you give it to her?"

"Yes."

"Hot damn." He squeezed her hand before releasing it. "You won't be sorry."

She prayed he was right.

19

Oksana had taken his advice. Lucky wanted to punch a fist in the air to celebrate, but he played it cool, instead. Time to back off and let things happen at their own pace.

As he and Oksana approached the porch steps, a sharp bark of welcome penetrated the massive front door.

"That's Sam, right?"

"Good memory considering you haven't seen him since August."

"He's a memorable dog. When I heard he's named after John Wayne's dog in *Hondo,* that made it stick. Perfect for Rowdy Ranch."

"We do have a theme going on."

"Tell me about it. Will I get to meet Silver while I'm here?"

"If you don't mind taking a walk in the cold."

"Doesn't bother this Montana girl. I'm used to—"

Sam barked again and the door swung open. His mom beckoned them forward. "Come in, come in! Sam's driving me nuts. He hasn't seen anybody but Andy and me all morning and he loves variety."

"I remember he was the life of the party at Marsh and Ella's reception." Once she was through the door, Oksana crouched in front of the collie and buried her fingers in his ruff. "How's my beautiful boy? How're you doing, Sam?"

The dog moaned happily and wiggled all over.

Lucky watched with envy in his heart as he put down her duffel and took off his jacket and hat. Oh, to be Sam. "You can tell he just hates that."

She laughed and scratched behind the collie's ears. "I miss having a dog. We have one at home, a mix of Lab and Golden Retriever. Daisy's a sweetheart, just like Sam."

Another piece of information he'd somehow missed. She was a dog lover. "Would you like to have one at the shop? I never thought to ask. Mom, would you object to that?"

"Not if they're well-behaved."

"It's a nice idea." Oksana stood and took off her red parka. "But I'm in no position to get a dog, much as I'd love to. I don't know where I'll end up after I graduate and it's much harder to find a place to rent if you have a pet."

"True." Reality slapped him in the face, and he needed that brisk smack. Of course she couldn't get a dog at this point in her life. "Let me take your parka." He hung it on the coat tree in the entry, a blaze of color against the tans and browns.

"I promise we'll set you up with a good workspace," his mom said. "I'm glad you decided to come out with the boys."

"Oh! We haven't told you. The power went out. I pretty much had to come."

"The whole town?" His mother's eyebrows rose. "Elvira will be—"

"Just us," he said. "It's more than a tripped breaker, so we need to get the electric company involved. I turned off the power and notified Wagon Train G&E."

"I hope it's not too dire, although we were going to close on Wednesday, anyway, for the wedding. When did it go out?"

"A few minutes after Rance showed up."

"It's a good thing he drove in to fetch you."

"A very good thing."

"If we can't get heat by tomorrow we'll have to drain the pipes. But enough about the shop. Have you two had anything to eat today?"

"We haven't. But you don't have to fix something, Mom. I'll do it."

"Then the kitchen's all yours. While you get started, I'll take Oksana to the kids' wing and let her choose where she'll be sleeping. I didn't make up a bed in advance so she can take her pick and help me make it up."

"Sounds like fun." Oksana looked his way. "I'll see if I can figure out which one was yours."

"Mine and Rance's. We shared."

"And you'd never find two boys more different, but it worked. Rance ramped things up and Lucky calmed them down." She gave him a fond glance. "Without you, Rance would have been a holy terror."

"And without Rance I wouldn't be here at all."

"I'm grateful you are." She gave his shoulder a squeeze. "Make whatever you want. We have plenty of eggs. Andy's building up the fire so you can eat in the living room."

"That sounds wonderful." Oksana picked up her duffel. "I haven't eaten in front of a real fire in a long time. Thank you for taking me in."

"I've been snowbound before and it can be lonely." She gestured toward the hallway.

"Sure can." Oksana fell into step beside her. "Happened to me in Missoula a few years ago."

They continued trading blizzard stories as they walked away. Sam trotted along behind, clearly thrilled to have a new friend.

Lucky gazed after them. Oksana had made a conquest by greeting the collie first thing. She was good with dogs. Good with people. Good with him.

His stomach rumbled, reminding him he'd offered to fix breakfast. He ducked through the arched doorway into the kitchen.

His mom had renovated it a few years ago, going for nostalgia. Cooking in it felt like a step back in time, except the retro appliances only looked old, with their rounded contours and pastel colors.

After putting on the coffee, he chopped and sauteed veggies he found in the fridge. Would Oksana take this opportunity to hand over her book? Probably not. That would be a little presumptuous when she'd just arrived.

She'd likely wait until she'd been here awhile. She'd have to find a time when Andy wasn't around. He added whisked eggs and scrambled everything together. After toasting English muffins and locating his favorite raspberry/rhubarb jam, he loaded one of his mom's largest trays.

Then he carried everything, including a generously sized carafe of coffee, into the living room. Andy was the only one there, sitting in one of the leather easy chairs by the fire reading the latest M.R. Morrison book.

He glanced up, took off his glasses and smiled. "Good to see you, son."

"You, too, Andy." He slowly lowered the heavy tray to the coffee table. "How about some coffee? I can bring you a mug."

"Thanks. I'll take you up on that."

Making tracks, Lucky was back in no time with two mugs in case his mother wanted some.

Andy used a scrap of paper to mark his place before he closed the book and laid it on the table. "Best one so far." He poured himself some coffee.

"I agree." Lucky sat on the couch catty-corner from Andy. "The reviewers seem to like the touch of romance. I'll bet you had something to do with Mom deciding to add that."

He chuckled, then lowered his voice. "Timing's wrong. She finished it last spring, before we got involved."

"I know, but we could all see it coming."

"Really? Wish you'd told me. I was prepared to get the bum's rush."

"Nah. She was on the same page as you. There was nobody else in the picture. Had to be you providing the inspiration for adding a little spice to the narrative."

"If that's the case, I can hardly wait for the next one."

Lucky grinned. "Think it'll make me blush?"

"Might. Could make me blush, too. But I say bring it on. Sex sells."

It tickled him to hear that from Andy, but it was true. "Might bring her new readers." He glanced toward the hallway before leaning closer to Andy. "Have you ever wondered if she's missing out by hiding her identity?"

"On what?"

"Enjoying her success in a more public way. Meeting her readers in person at a signing. Sure, she can look at reviews, but we're the only people she physically hears praise from — her family and the Wenches. She has thousands of fans who would love to speak to M.R. Morrison."

"Hm. Hadn't thought about that. I sure enjoy it when people stop me on the street to thank me for my column or mention a particular part that made 'em laugh."

"See? You're proving the point."

"Of course, sometimes they ding me for an opinion they don't agree with, but that's okay, too. It's nice to get personal feedback. What made you think of it?"

"I didn't. Oksana brought it up. She's been trying to get in touch with M.R. Morrison so she can talk him into doing a signing at the bookshop."

"Did you tell her that's unlikely?"

"Yes, and that's when she described how great it would be when all his fans showed up to shower him with compliments. Mom's never had that experience."

"I'd be interested to hear what she has to say about it. But not now. Here they come." He stood.

So did Lucky. It was how he'd been raised.

His mom and Oksana walked over and took seats, his mom in the easy chair across the coffee table from Andy and Oksana on the couch near the food.

"It looks and smells delicious, Lucky." She sent him a quick smile.

"Then dig in." He lifted one of the mugs. "Mom? Coffee?"

"Yes, please."

He poured it and Oksana passed it over. Then they both dived into their breakfast.

Since he couldn't ask about the manuscript, he chose the next most interesting topic. "Which room did you pick?"

"Angie's old room because it's the one with the bunks."

"Excellent."

His mom looked at him. "It's a mystery to me why they're so popular."

"Because they're cool." He glanced at Oksana. "Right?"

"Absolutely."

"Rance and I hated giving them to Angie, but we'd turned ten. We'd aged out."

"I found all three of your initials carved into the bed posts."

"There are ten sets of those if you know where to look."

His mother let out a beleaguered sigh. "Those beds are pug-ugly, but since you guys all seem to love them, evidently they're here to stay."

"They're not ugly, Mom. They have character."

"Which is a nice way of saying they're covered in nicks, scratches and splotches of paint. If Clint refinished them, at least they'd be—"

"*Refinish* them? You're kidding, right?"

"Why not? They're solid wood, so he could take a power sander to them and add a light stain. Then they'd look halfway decent."

"Clint won't agree to it."

"Then I'll hire somebody."

"Before you do, I'd like to request a family meeting."

She rolled her eyes. "About the bunk beds."

"Yes, ma'am. I know technically they belong to you, and you can do whatever you want with them, but at least let us present our side."

She shifted her attention to Andy. "Have you seen those bunks? I mean, really examined them?"

"Yes, I have."

"Will you back me up, here?"

"Sorry, Dez. I agree with Lucky. The bunks should stay as is. They're a piece of history, something your kids can show our grandkids."

"So they can be taught that defacing furniture is a good thing?"

"No, so we can let them know this is the *only* time it's allowed. The bunks are special, a family heirloom."

"Heirloom?"

"That's what I'm saying. Soon Mav and Zach will be big enough to sleep in them when they spend the night, and you know they'll want to. When they're old enough to use a pocketknife, we can help them carve their initials, just like their fathers did."

His mom shuddered. "I didn't know that was going on back in the day and I don't want to know now. You can handle the pocketknife situation. I want nothing to do with it."

"That's exactly the kind of thing grandpas are good for." He raised his mug in her direction before taking a sip.

Lucky smiled at him. "Thanks, Andy." Then he took a peek at Oksana to see what she thought of the exchange. She was focused on him, her gaze warm and... loving. No mistaking the emotion shining in her eyes.

For a moment he let himself soak it in. Then he looked away. Her life was in flux, and he was a much bigger gamble than a dog.

_20_

The main house at Rowdy Ranch had wrapped Oksana in a hug from the moment she'd stepped inside. After a few hours spent studying by the fire, she wanted to stay forever.

Earlier she'd helped clean up the breakfast dishes in the delightfully retro kitchen. Then Rance had stopped by to give Lucky a ride home so he could _wash the stink off_, as Rance put it. Those two made her laugh.

Desiree had generously given her several options for her study session. The library had dazzled her with its shelves full of classics and rainbow of wingback chairs, but she'd have been tempted to browse the shelves instead of taking the multiple-choice exam waiting on her laptop.

The huge dining table would have provided room to spread out and she'd also briefly considered setting up in Rowdy Roost. Working at the antique bar had been appealing.

But the warmth of a crackling fire had won out, especially since Desiree had offered her a lap desk and Andy had committed to tending the fire while he finished the newest M.R. Morrison book. Oksana had finished it a couple of days ago and looked forward to discussing it with him when he was done.

Desiree had excused herself to chat with Angie about a few wedding details and had disappeared into the bedroom she shared with Andy. She hadn't come back, so maybe she'd had other calls to make. She might have a home office there, too.

If so, she hadn't offered that space as a study area. Not that it would have been preferable to this cozy fireplace venue. Oksana was in danger of being spoiled for her little electric one.

About the time she was ready to take a break, Sam got up from his bed near the fire and raced down the hall to the entryway, nails clicking. Moments later Lucky and Rance came through the door, their voices subdued.

Was something wrong? She closed her laptop and waited for them to walk into the living room. Instead they detoured into the kitchen and opened the fridge, still talking in muted tones.

The sound of their boots on the wood floor faded away to her right, in the direction of Rowdy Roost. Sam returned and plopped down on his bed with a sigh.

"They probably went to play pool."

She turned toward Andy.

He'd pushed his glasses to the top of his head and was regarding her with amusement. "You said you needed to work, so they're trying not to disturb you."

"But this is their house, and the fire is lovely. I don't want to keep them from enjoying it just because I decided to study here."

"Are you ready for a break?"

"As a matter of fact, I am."

"Then go on out there and let them know, although they'll probably want to finish their game."

"I will." Setting the laptop desk aside, she stood and stretched.

Andy got to his feet, too. "I'll go check on Dez, see if she wants me to start lunch."

She glanced at the book he'd laid down. "Finished?"

"Still have a couple of chapters to go."

"And you can just put it down? I couldn't."

"I already know how it ends."

"You peeked?"

He chuckled. "You could say that."

"Okay." She gave a little shrug. "No judgment."

"None taken. Tell the boys we'll be having lunch soon and not to load up on cider and chips."

"Oh, I'm sure they'll listen to me. Should I wag my finger in their faces while I say that?"

Laughter sparkled in his eyes. "Couldn't hurt. I'm glad you came out today, Oksana. You're a pleasure to have around."

"Thank you. And thank you for keeping me company and minding the fire."

"Anytime. See you in a few." He gave the fire a quick glance before walking toward the open bedroom door.

She turned and went in the opposite direction. She'd been curious about why Desiree had proposed to Andy after avoiding matrimony for so long. The answer was obvious. He was a find.

The crack of one pool ball hitting another confirmed Andy's prediction. She stepped softly, trying to sneak up on them. Holding her breath, she peered over the louvered barroom doors.

Only the light fixture above the pool table was on. The focused beams created highlights in Lucky's dark curls as he leaned over to line up a shot. Then he paused and lifted his head. "Hey there. Come on in."

She looked into eyes that matched the felt table covering. Even though she'd been quiet, he must have sensed her. Right on cue, her heart raced and her palms grew sweaty. She pushed through the swinging doors. "Don't let me interrupt."

"Oh, please interrupt." Rance waved his bottle of cider in the air. "He's whipping my butt. My ego can't take much more."

"I guess it's my Lucky day." With a grin, he sent another ball into the pocket.

His smile brought her attention to his beard. He'd neatened it up. No question about it, Lucky McLintock was a handsome devil.

"And then he adds insult to injury by making that creaky old joke. Now I suppose he'll run the table."

"That's my plan." He straightened, picked up the chalk and twisted it over the tip of his cue. "But first I need to ask how the studying's going."

"Great. I'm taking a break and Andy should be fixing lunch soon. You're not supposed to fill up on cider and chips." She checked out the collapsed chip bag on a nearby table and a cider bottle that was nearly empty. "I see I'm too late."

"No worries." Rance tipped his bottle and polished off the last few swallows. "Lucky and me, we can always eat. Did you say Andy's fixing lunch?"

"Sounded that way."

"Oh, that's right. Sunday's his day to cook. He's way better at it than Mom, but don't tell her I said so."

"She'd agree with you." Lucky sent another ball into the pocket. "She's never claimed to be a great cook. That's one of the reasons we have Marybeth."

"And now we also have Andy. I admire a man who can cook. Like Lucky, here."

"How about you, Rance?" She chose to focus on the brother who wasn't giving her heart palpitations. "Can you cook?"

"It's not my jam. I'm too easily distracted. I can't even boil an egg. It usually ends up exploding because I've forgotten all about it. I rock at cleanup, though." He turned and surveyed the table. "And here he goes. I'm toast."

Lucky moved quickly after that, sending the last few balls flying into pockets and finishing up by neatly tapping in the eight ball.

"Burritos are ready!" Andy's voice boomed out. "Come and get 'em while they're hot!"

Rance whooped with joy. "That's what I'm talkin' 'bout. Give me your cue, Lucky, and rack up the balls." He snapped the cues into the holder on the wall. "Those burritos won't eat themselves."

"Head on in, bro. We'll be right behind you. I just need to check with Oksana. She was going to look up something for me while she was online."

"I was?"

"Yeah, you know. The thing."

"I don't remember a—"

"You two hash it out." Rance gave them a wave and pushed through the swinging doors. "I'm getting me a piping hot burrito to eat in front of the fire."

Lucky put a hand on her arm. "The manuscript," he murmured. "Have you given it to her?"

"Not yet. She left the room to call Angie about wedding stuff and never came back out. Plus Andy was right there, and I'd left it in my room."

"Ah. Okay. I wondered, because we never discussed whether you were going to say asking her was my idea or yours, and I've been thinking about which is better."

"Does that matter?"

"Well, if she doesn't know I've read it and liked it, you may get a more objective opinion, which is what you're after."

"Then you think I should say this was all my idea?"

"No, I don't. Despite what I just said, let's tell her the truth. That's a more honest approach."

She gasped. "All of it?"

"No, no. Not the truth about us. Just about the book."

"Whew." She pressed a hand to her chest, where her heart was thumping like crazy. "You scared me a little."

"Sorry, didn't mean to. Anyway, knowing I'm the one who suggested giving it to her will make her expect to like it, but she's an old hand at this. She'll put that aside once she's into it."

"Assuming I can find a time to give it to her."

He gazed at her. "Are you having second thoughts?"

"No. I've just never been good at cloak and dagger stuff."

"Then maybe I can help create an opportunity. And by the way, Rance wants us to spend the night over here. He's feeling nostalgic for the old days."

"Then you'll be here until tomorrow morning?"

"Afraid so. I couldn't figure out a way to avoid it without disappointing him."

"I understand. We'll—"

"Hey, you two." Desiree came through the swinging doors. "Is there something wrong at the shop that you're not telling me?"

Oksana sucked in a breath at the same time Lucky did. Then they both said *No* with unnecessary emphasis.

"There is, isn't there? I got suspicious when Rance told me you'd asked Oksana to look something up online. Then I came back here and find you two with your heads together, clearly trying to sort through an issue. Out with it."

"It's not the shop," Lucky said. "The shop's fine."

"I wrote a book, Desiree. Actually, I've written—"

"A book? What kind?" Her expression shifted immediately from irritation to intense curiosity.

"It's fiction aimed at girls aged ten or eleven through maybe sixteen. I—"

"I've read most of it, Mom, and it's great. Really—"

"Is it here?"

"Yes. I convinced Oksana to bring it and ask if you'd read it."

His mother frowned.

Oh, no. She was going to refuse. Oksana's throat tightened. "I know you're busy, and now is not the time. There's Angie's wedding, but—"

"You don't have to rush to read it," Lucky said. "Her mom's the only one besides me she's shown it to. It's not like she's ready to publish—"

"Be quiet for a minute, son." Desiree gave him a long look. "Why did you tell her my opinion is worth seeking?"

"Because you're the one who started the Wenches Who Read, and after all these years of evaluating books, you've got a handle on whether a story works or not."

Her shoulders relaxed. "I suppose that's true." She turned back to Oksana. "So where is this book?"

"In my room. I mean, in the room where I'm—"

"I know what you mean, sweetheart. I'm guessing you don't want anyone else to know about it."

"Not yet. I wasn't planning to show it to Lucky, but that just sort of happened. And he suggested—"

"Giving it to me. I'm sure bringing it here took courage."

"I was scared to death. Still am."

"I understand that more than you know. I'll agree to read it and keep it to myself on one condition. I have no secrets from Andy. I won't let him read it, but I will tell him what I'm doing. You'll have to be okay with that."

"I'm okay with that. I know I can trust him."

Desiree smiled. "He has that effect on people."

"Thank you, Desiree. Thank you so much. Like I told Lucky, I want the truth."

"I would give you no less. Now let's go get those yummy burritos."

Dragging in a breath, she followed Desiree through the swinging doors. Behind her, Lucky reached out and gave her shoulder a squeeze.

The request hadn't been made the way she would have chosen, but it had been made. And granted. Desiree would soon meet Odette Bidelspach. The rest was up to Odette.

21

Having a mom who was a good storyteller sure came in handy. Lucky managed to keep a straight face as she told a big wooly about Oksana's online search to see if he could arrange prepaid surfing lessons for Angie and Dallas on Oahu.

"That's a great idea," Rance said. "I heard Angie say some things would have to wait for the next trip. Did you find anything, Oksana?"

"I'm working on it."

"Let me know. I'll chip in."

"I'll cover it, bro." Lucky had to put a stop to this. "You've already contributed—"

"No, *I'll* cover it." His mother sent them both a look that meant the discussion was over. "I wish I'd thought of surfing lessons."

Which she had. He grabbed his napkin to cover a grin.

"You and Rance have been more than generous. Everyone has, including the Armstrongs."

"Speaking of those folks," Andy said. "What's the word on their flights?"

"I talked to Vanessa this morning. Flights are snarled up all over, including Newark. They're scheduled to come in Tuesday."

"Tuesday?" Andy held her gaze. "That's cutting it close."

"It's the best they can do since they have weather issues, too. They gain time coming west, so they should make it for the rehearsal and the rehearsal dinner. And the wedding, which is the main thing."

Rance snorted. "I told Angie if she was determined to marry a Jersey guy, she needed to wait until it warmed up. But did she listen to me? No, she did not, and here we are."

"At least Wednesday's supposed to be nice." His mom picked up her empty plate and stood. "Which always seems to happen on her birthday. Andy, those burritos were yummy."

"Thanks." He got up, too, prompting the rest to do the same and echo his mom's comment about the burritos.

"Have the boys told you they're staying overnight?"

"Hadn't heard that. My lasagna should feed us all, though. And since you're both staying, you can help me make it."

"Works for me," Lucky said.

"I don't think you want me in there, Andy." Rance grabbed his plate off the coffee table and began collecting the others, including the one his mother was holding. "Ask Mom and Lucky. I'm a cooking disaster. But I'll gladly be the cleanup crew. I'll start with these lunch dishes."

"If you can't cook, how do you feed yourself, son?"

"That's where my job at the Buffalo comes in. If I work a double shift, I get lunch and dinner."

"That still leaves sizeable gaps in your eating schedule."

"Fortunately I know how to open a jar of peanut butter and take sliced bread out of the wrapper."

"I'd love to help cook tonight, Andy," Oksana said. "That kitchen's awesome."

"I appreciate the offer, but I believe it's Rance's turn. I know for a fact he intends to get hitched someday. Any woman worth her salt will expect him to know his way around the kitchen." He eyed Rance. "Am I right?"

"You make a good point, sir. But I—"

"Have you heard the term *willful ignorance*?"

Lucky hid a smile. Rance was not wiggling out of this one.

"No, but I can guess what it means." He held Andy's gaze. "I'll help cook tonight. It'll be my pleasure."

"Thank you. Now let's get those plates into the dishwasher."

"Yes, sir." He lengthened his stride on the way to the kitchen.

Exchanging a quick glance of solidarity with his mother, Lucky pressed his lips together to keep from laughing.

"Nicely done, my love." She smiled at Andy.

"Wasn't sure I'd get away with it."

"He respects you and he's finding out you won't put up with his BS."

"But it's true that he's easily distracted," Lucky said. "I've seen the results in his kitchen."

"I'll keep my eye on him."

His mom nodded. "Good. Hey, Oksana, I forgot to give you an extra blanket when we made your bed. It'll be cold tonight. Let's go take care of that."

His mom didn't forget about blankets. Lucky knew better. She wasn't big on cooking but she made sure everyone was cozy and warm. While the men were in the kitchen, she'd have a chance to spirit Oksana's manuscript from the kids' wing over to her office.

Sure enough, when he came back into the living room to get a couple of water glasses they'd missed, she was hurrying toward her bedroom, the manuscript tucked under her arm.

She paused when she saw him. "Is that all you told her? Just the part about the Wenches?"

"Yes, ma'am. And thank you for doing this."

"You're welcome. Also, she mentioned that she's hoping to get a tour of the barn so she can meet Silver."

His pulse rate picked up. Was Oksana deliberately creating alone time? He should nix that for both their sakes. He wasn't going to. "We talked about it."

"If you're going, you should do it now. Another hour and the temperature will start dipping."

"You're right. Is she still back there?"

"Uh-huh. Searching for the rest of the initials."

He squirmed a little. "Listen, about those bunks, I—"

"Don't worry. I'm not upset with you. You stood up for something that's part of your history, like Andy said. I don't know if I'd call it an heirloom, but maybe it is."

"Andy's good for this family."

"Yes, he is." She cocked her head to listen as laughter erupted in the kitchen. "And especially for Rance." She looked down at the manuscript under her arm. "I'd better go tuck this away and check into surfing lessons. Go find Oksana." She hurried through the recently constructed bedroom door.

Part of your history. He hadn't thought of the bunk beds that way, but they were. Beau had started the initials thing before Lucky and Rance were born. Then his big brother had supervised the carving when they'd turned seven, the magic age for pocketknives.

Not for Angie, though. She'd pestered the entire family for a solid year and got hers at six. He chuckled as he walked back to the kids' wing. That girl lived a charmed life. Because of Oksana's book project, she'd get her surfing lessons. His mom would see to it.

He found Oksana lying on her back shining her phone flashlight under the bottom bunk.

"None of them are under there."

"Are you sure? I've looked everywhere for Sky's. He's the only one I can't find."

"Because he didn't make it easy. Beau had to talk him into doing it. Sky was sure they'd get in big trouble."

"Did they?" She scooted out and sat up. "I doubt your mom was thrilled."

"She didn't notice. Too busy. By the time somebody blabbed, the tradition was established. Angie's dad Gene was here at the time, and according to Sky, his reaction was a lot like Andy's."

"I was impressed with how you defended these bunks."

"Any of us would have done the same. Want to keep hunting for Sky's initials?"

"Nah. Enough's enough. Where are they?"

He held out his hand. "Hop up and I'll show you."

She let him pull her to her feet, and for a moment he held on, tempted to kiss her.

Nope. Not here. He let go. "It's on the back of that top left-hand post. With the bed pushed against the wall, it's impossible to find."

"Good thing I gave up."

"I'll pull the bed out." He grabbed a post.

"That's okay. I don't have to see it."

"You've come this far. Might as well finish the quest." He pulled hard and the heavy bed moved a couple of inches. He yanked again and gained another inch. "Now you should be able to see it."

Walking to the end of the bed, she pressed her cheek against the wall. "There it is. *SM*." She stepped back. "Thanks."

"You bet." Bracing his shoulder against the post, he pushed it back in one go. "Heavy sucker."

"Which begs the question. How did two young boys get it far enough from the wall for Sky to carve his initials?"

"I never thought of that, but they would have needed help." He did the math. "It had to be Gene. He was a woodworker. I'll bet he was in on it, probably helped when Clint and Cheyenne wanted to do theirs. No wonder he defended the program."

"This place is full of stories, isn't it?"

"Yes, ma'am." Seeing it through her eyes made him more aware of that than he'd ever been. He still wanted to kiss her, so he'd better move on with the program before he put their secret in jeopardy. "Mom said you still want to meet Silver and the gang. Buck and Sky kept the horses in today so it's easier to eyeball the whole group."

"Do you have the time?"

"I'm loaded with time." He wrapped a hand around the bed post so he wouldn't wrap it around her. "You're the one who has work to do."

"I got most of it done. Another hour and I'll be caught up. I have time for a barn tour, but you must be dead on your feet."

"I took a nap after my shower. That should hold me until bedtime." His breath hitched. "You'd better stop looking at me like that."

"Sorry." She glanced away.

"Not that I don't love it, but—"

"Let's go to the barn. Where we can talk."

"Is that what we'll do?"

Her breathless laugh gave him the answer and his groin tightened.

Five minutes later they trudged through ankle-deep snow to the barn, fogging the air as they talked.

"Sky and Beau sound like you and Rance, the cautious one and the impulsive one."

"Rance definitely takes after Beau. He's idolized the guy for years, used to copy the way Beau walks. I wish I could say I'm like Sky. He's got it together."

"He's also older than you."

"Only by six years."

"But think of where you could be in six years. You might have an additional two or even three bookshops by then, with managers working under you, and—"

"I thought about that while I was at my cabin. I got a little carried away talking about it last night."

"And I loved hearing the enthusiasm in your voice. It's a neat idea."

"But now's not the time to bring it up. There's Angie's wedding, and the Armstrongs will be staying on after the newlyweds fly to Hawaii. And Mom's got a—" Whoa. He almost said *deadline*. He was getting way too comfy with Oksana. "She's got a lot on her plate. I need to wait until things settle down."

"Correct me if I'm wrong, but does it ever completely settle down?"

"Well...."

"I'm only a bystander, but from my vantage point you have pockets of calm, like this morning when I was studying, Andy was reading and your mom had some calls to make. But in the wider view, something big is always going on with your family."

"I suppose that's accurate."

"In other words, if you're waiting for all the big things to get handled before you broach this, it's never gonna happen."

He chewed on that for a while. "I take your point, but I still want to wait until after the wedding is over and the Armstrongs have left."

"Which is certainly your choice to make."

"But you think it's the wrong one."

"Oh, Lucky." She sighed. "I just want you to move forward with your dreams."

Sadness lay heavy on his chest. What good was a dream if it didn't include her?

22

Frustrating. Oksana had adored Lucky ever since she'd interviewed for the job. She'd also wondered if he had any ambitions beyond managing L'Amour and More. After eighteen months of working with him, she'd concluded he was content where he was.

Nothing wrong with that. Not everyone had big goals. But now that Lucky had revealed his, she'd become invested. And something was holding him back.

Was it any of her business? No. Could she let it drop? She vowed to try. As they neared the barn, she gave it a shot. "Listen, forget what I just said. I can be pushy and think I know best. You need to do things at your own pace."

"You mean slow as molasses?" He slid the barn door open and motioned her in.

"I didn't mean to imply that."

"I know. But I get what you're saying."

"And I promise not to bring it up again." She breathed in the earthy scents of a working barn. "Smells better in here than I expected."

"Buck and Sky can't tolerate a smelly barn. We're on a rotation for mucking stalls, especially now that Buck's getting on in years."

"Everybody?" The barn was warm. Flipping back her hood, she unzipped her jacket.

"That's right. Mom, Andy, everyone except Cheyenne and Kendall, since he lives over at her place, now." He unbuttoned his jacket. "We each take a shift. If you ride, you rake. It's only fair."

"That's a lot of help."

"It's also a lot of horses. We'll outgrow this barn soon, the way things are going. " He made no attempt to hold her hand or steal a kiss.

Likely her fault for urging him to talk to his mother about the expansion. "How far away is Silver?"

"Down at the far end, but you're welcome to visit some of the others along the way."

"I will, then." She was drawn to a sweet-looking buckskin named Buttermilk, who occupied a stall next to a striking palomino named Trigger. "The nameplates are a nice touch."

"Mom's idea."

"I should've guessed." The buckskin mare hung her head over the stall door and closed her eyes when Oksana scratched behind her ears. "Trigger and Buttermilk. How many people would get the significance of those names?"

"Quite a few in Wagon Train. Even the kids, now that you can easily get Roy Rogers and Dale Evans on TV. I grew up watching those old shows." Lucky walked over and stroked the palomino's neck.

"Me, too." She'd never have imagined they'd be alone in the barn caressing horses instead of each other. But she wouldn't make the first move.

"Trigger's now the senior member of this crew. After Mom got Trigger, she decided to search for other famous lookalikes. Dollor over there, Gil's horse, is the spitting image of the one John Wayne insisted on riding in his last few movies."

"And who's this chocolate beauty with the creamy mane and tail?" She checked the nameplate. "Hi, there, Koko. You're a gorgeous boy." She rubbed under his chin.

"He's Clint's, a lookalike for Rex Allen's horse."

"Rex Allen. I'd forgotten him. I need to brush up on my Western heroes and horses."

A nicker from the end of the barn made Lucky smile. "We'd better go see Silver and catch the others on the way back. He's getting impatient for some attention."

So was she, but she wasn't about to say so.

He sauntered down toward the white horse and rubbed his nose. "Didn't mean to ignore you, bud. The lady's never been here and I didn't want to rush her through the tour." He turned toward her. "Come say hello to Silver."

When she moved in to rub Silver's nose, Lucky stepped back to give her room. "Hey, Silver." She scratched under his white mane. "You're spectacular. I'll bet you disappear in the snow."

"He almost does. There's not a speck of black or brown on him."

"Did you want a white horse?"

"Sure did. I was a Lone Ranger fan as a kid. Had the mask, white hat, even make-believe silver bullets."

"What about now? Do you ever dress up?"

"Take a guess."

"No?"

"Rance keeps trying to get me to do it for the Fourth of July parade, but it's not my style. I offered to trade horses so he could be the Lone Ranger, but Diablo gets more attention from the ladies so he doesn't want to trade."

"Ah, Diablo. I see him over there. Nothing as dramatic as a black and white Paint. Whose horse was that?"

"Cisco Kid."

"Right. It's coming back to me. My dad has a comic book collection from that era. I was allowed to look at them if I was very careful."

"I'm sure you were."

"Absolutely. He cherishes those old comics." She looked back down the aisle. "Are they all named after Hollywood horses?"

He chuckled. "Hollywood horses. I like that. Makes me picture them wearing sunglasses and prancing down a red carpet."

"Works for me. They're amazing."

"So are you." The words were soft, but he'd dropped the casual tone.

She turned and met his intense gaze. A quiver ran through her body.

Closing the gap between them, he drew her into his arms. "You're incredible. You have more talent in your little finger than I have in my whole body."

"That's not true. You—"

"It is true. You know what you want and you'll get it. You'll succeed beyond your wildest dreams. And so help me God, I won't get in your way."

"I know you won't." The quiver grew stronger, making her shake. "Anyway, you have your own dreams. You have the same potential to—"

"Oksana." His tucked her in closer. "I need to kiss you one last time. And tell you how much the past twenty-four hours have meant to me."

She gulped. "I don't want it to end."

"I know. Neither do I. But it has to. You're going places, and I... I don't know what my future holds."

"*Lucky.*" She gripped the collar of his jacket. "You *do* know. You have a vision of—"

"And you listened." He dipped his head, his mouth hovering over hers. "That means the world to me. I'll never forget the way you made me feel. You have a gift."

"*You're* the gift. If only—"

"Shhh." His lips came down on hers with a tenderness that broke her heart. His kiss was filled with warmth and gratitude. Heat simmered in the background but never intruded.

He kissed her slowly, with infinite care, his mouth gentle, his breathing in time with hers. Tears pricked the back of her eyes.

No doubt about it. Lucky was kissing her goodbye.

23

Lucky held Oksana close for as long as he dared. After this, he would never hold her again. Could he manage to work alongside her for the next ten months without going crazy? Stupid question. He had to.

When his body's responses threatened to ruin his good intentions, he slowly let her go and backed away. But he held her gaze, even though the sadness in her dark eyes tore him up.

He had many flaws. But cowardice wasn't one of them. "You're hurting. And I'm sorry about that."

"You're hurting, too, and I'm the one who should be sorry. I started this. I asked you to kiss me before you went down to Bret and Gil's shop."

"And I could have said no. I could have slept on that bedroll downstairs. And even though this part is tough, I don't regret making the decisions I did."

She opened her mouth, as if to say something more. Then she closed it and took a deep breath. "Neither do I. You've set a high bar, though, Lucky McLintock."

"Backatcha, Oksana Jones." He dragged in a breath. "We should probably go back to the house."

"Probably." She didn't move.

Looked like he'd have to. He started down the aisle. "You have another hour of work for your classes and I promised Rance I'd give him a shot at evening the score with another game of pool."

She fell into step beside him. "You're pretty good at that."

"Haven't always been, since my brothers got a head start. But after Mom added on Rowdy Roost and bought a pool table, I practiced every chance I got. It's something you can do by yourself."

"I hadn't thought of that, but you're right. Would you say you're the best pool player in the family?"

"Maybe. Rance is pretty good. Practice makes a big difference. The pool table showed up a little late for everybody except Rance and me."

"Why? Don't you all play?"

"We do, but since we're still single, we have more time to work on our game. By now we can take anyone in the family." He couldn't figure out where she was heading with this, so he decided to turn it into a joke. "Think I should give up the bookstore job and turn pro?"

"Not at all. I just—" She glanced over at him. "You're kidding."

"Yep. I like pool but I love books — reading them, talking about them, the feel of them in my hands, the look of them on a shelf."

"Ever wanted to write one?"

"No. I'll leave that to you and my—" He stopped in time, thank God. "My favorite authors." He swallowed. Close one.

After years of keeping his mother's secret, he was having trouble keeping it from Oksana. Made sense. He wanted her to know.

That was his end game, and he might as well admit it. Maybe his mom would critique her book and leave it at that. But if she really wanted to be a mentor, she'd have to reveal who she was.

He wanted Oksana to have the full benefit of his mother's standing in the industry. With her contacts, she could eliminate the barriers that most first-time authors faced.

Would his mom agree that Oksana's talent merited that? He prayed she would.

A few feet short of the closed barn doors, she stopped. "Before we go back, I want to say something."

"I have a hunch it's about my expansion project."

"Would you rather not hear it?"

"Are you gonna say I should corner my mother when we get back?"

"No."

"Okay, then."

She faced him. "What you said about your love of books just now was wonderful. If anyone can make a success of the idea, you can. Think of the joy you could bring Apple Grove by opening a bookshop."

"Assuming Trent's research says they want one and would buy books there."

"But his research won't take you into account. You're the secret sauce."

"Me? Nah."

"You're so wrong. Your enthusiasm is catching. And customers trust you because you're one of them, a Montana-born cowboy who was raised on a ranch."

His breath hitched. Montana-born purely by accident. But he didn't say it. She was on a roll.

"What if you went to Apple Grove and chatted with the people there?"

"Just accost them on the street?"

"No, but you said your mom has a connection to the town."

"She does. Sky does, too."

"Great. If the McLintocks are known there, so much the better."

"I'm not going to trade on—"

"Why not? Take Rance. Two strapping McLintocks will make more of an impression than one. Do they have a gathering place like the Buffalo?"

"Sky and Beau mentioned the Choosy Moose."

That made her smile. "Sounds like an excellent venue. You can stop in and show folks pictures of this shop and let them know the kind of cozy Western atmosphere they'll enjoy."

He took a deep breath and sorted through what she'd said. Visiting the town himself made sense. Maybe Rance would be an asset. Taking pictures of the shop to show customers at the local watering hole might work.

But he wasn't about to toss around the McLintock name as if he had a right to do that. The shop was something he could point to with pride, though. He'd put ten years into it and was proud of the balance sheets for those years.

He chose to start with a positive comment. "I like the idea of taking some pictures and dropping in at the Choosy Moose."

"Good. Me, too."

"I still need to get the all-clear from Mom before I ever set foot in Apple Grove."

"I know." She looked him in the eye, clearly waiting for what she had to know was coming.

"I'm not bothering her with it until things settle down."

She held his gaze for a beat. Then she hit him with a zinger. "You bothered her with my manuscript."

"That's different."

"How?"

"It just is." Lamest response in the world.

Her expression softened. "Because that was for someone else, and this is for you?"

He glanced away. "Let it go, Oksana." He admired her dogged persistence. It would take her far in this world. But he didn't appreciate that quality right now.

"What if you mentioned the idea to Rance?"

His attention snapped back to her. "What? Hell, no!"

"Why not? You said he could be trusted not to blab things he's not supposed to. Listen, you talked me into getting another opinion on my book, so I'm urging you to get another opinion on this project."

He blinked. "Those two things are entirely different."

"You'll have to explain that to me, because I don't think they're different at all. My stomach cramps up when I think of your mother reading my book."

"It does?" Guilt pricked him. "I'm sorry. I didn't realize—"

"But then I tell myself that I eventually want it published and giving it to a perceptive reader is another step in the process."

"Okay, but I don't see how sharing my idea with Rance is another step in the process."

"It will be if he likes it."

"Why? He can't give me permission to open another L'Amour and More bookshop in Apple Grove."

"But he might help you see it's not as big a deal as you think it is to discuss it with your mom."

"Which it wouldn't be for him. You're right, he'd just tell me to dive right in, because that's what he'd do in my place."

"And you think he'd be making a mistake to dive right in? That he'd cause a problem?"

"Not necessarily. If it felt right to him, it would probably work out just fine. But I'm not him."

"You're pretty darn close. You're brothers, born within hours of each other."

His gut tightened. She didn't understand his position, even though he'd told her about his penniless mother who'd given birth under an alias and his nameless father who'd left without a trace.

Then again, he couldn't expect her to understand. He couldn't expect any of the siblings he'd acquired with the stroke of a pen to understand, either.

They all knew who their parents were and why they looked like they did. His green eyes, his curly hair, the shape of his nose — no one in the wonderful family he'd fallen into shared any of his features. He didn't look like any of them.

Despite the name he'd been given when Desiree had adopted him twenty-eight years ago, he wasn't a McLintock.

24

Oksana couldn't read Lucky's expression. He'd closed down, and his silence likely meant he wouldn't take her suggestion and talk to Rance.

His deep sigh wasn't encouraging, either. "I'll think about it."

"Okay. I'll stop badgering you."

"I know you mean well." He reached for the latch on the door and slid it open. Air much colder than it had been earlier swept in.

She gasped as it blew her parka open. She struggled to zip it.

"Sorry!" Quickly closing the door, he buttoned his coat and turned up the collar. "Got distracted. Ready?"

"Sure."

He opened the door again, letting in the bitter cold again. "Come here." Wrapping a protective arm around her shoulders, he stepped out and kept a grip on her as he turned and slid the door closed.

If he was willing to share his body warmth on the way back to the house, she wouldn't object. She was seldom out in weather like this now that she lived and worked in the same place.

He tucked her against his side as they hurried across the open space. So close and yet so far. After this she'd have no excuse to cuddle with him. Although the icy breeze made her face hurt, and smoke from a cedar fire teased her with the promise of a crackling blaze, she hated reaching the porch steps.

Their ascent wasn't very coordinated. The steps were more slippery than they had been. Or maybe she was less sure-footed because she was thinking about the moment when they'd arrive at the door and he'd let her go.

And he did, pausing to knock the snow off his boots. She quickly cleaned hers as he reached for the doorknob and Sam barked a welcome.

A knife twisted in her chest. She'd not only fallen for the guy, she'd fallen for his family, the home where he'd been raised, and the family dog.

The moment she was inside and unzipped her parka, she crouched down and hugged Sam, burying her cold face in the collie's soft ruff. Sam moaned and wriggled with happiness.

"I think he likes you a little bit."

She lifted her head. Lucky's wistful expression brought her to her feet, a lump in her throat. "I screwed up. I never should have allowed my harmless crush to get out of con—"

"Hey, Rance, Oksana and Lucky are back." Andy came down the hall from the living room. "We need to make the lasagna. It needs time to bake ."

"Let me take your jacket." Lucky slipped it from her shoulders, leaning in, his voice low. "Don't beat yourself up. We'll be fine."

"Right." She'd keep telling herself that, but the longing in his green eyes just now said he was in for some grief.

Leaving her wet boots in the entryway, she padded in her stocking feet back to the living room. Desiree sat in the same easy chair she'd taken this morning at breakfast. Reading glasses perched on her nose, her furry slippers propped on the coffee table, she concentrated on a large book lying in her lap.

She didn't look up. Oksana hadn't made any noise and the crackling fire likely masked the sound of Sam's nails on the hardwood as he'd followed her in.

Something about that book in her lap was odd. It looked like… no, it couldn't be. But it was. She'd found a dustcover from an oversized hardback and taped it to the binder for *The Life and Times of Odette Bidelspach.*

Oh, hell, no. Giving the book to Desiree was one thing. Sitting in the same room with her while she read it was a whole other level of torture.

If she could quietly pick up her laptop, she might be able to tiptoe to her room and work there. She'd left it to recharge on the end table next to what seemed to be Andy's usual chair. He'd found her an extension cord and she'd been able to hook up to a wall outlet.

Could she creep around to the laptop, unplug it, then make it all the way back around the couch, past Desiree and escape through the dining room to the kids' wing? Sam stood watching her, tail wagging slowly, tongue hanging from the side of his mouth, as if he couldn't wait to see how this turned out.

Moving carefully, she edged around Sam, her body hunched over as if that would somehow make her less visible. It wouldn't, but it felt like the right way to sneak.

She monitored her breathing as she took one slow step at a time. Sam kept the same measured pace, her silent partner as they passed the easy chair. The laptop was within reach.

Leaning down, she worked the connection free, making sure there was no pop or click at the end. Then she laid the cord gently on the floor.

Not a sound from Desiree. She must be deeply engrossed in the book. Either that, or she'd fallen asleep. That was a depressing thought.

Clutching the laptop and still hunched over, Oksana made her way past Andy's chair again. She could do this. The hard part was over. She was almost—

Desiree snorted with laughter.

Was she laughing at something in the book? Watching someone crack up over a scene in the book would be awesome. She couldn't resist looking.

Desiree looked right back, grinning. "Sorry. I was going to let you escape, but you and Sam were too funny. He was slinking along like he knew exactly what was required."

Face hot, she straightened. "I, um, didn't want to disturb you."

"And I have to apologize. I thought I could get a few pages read while you and Lucky were out at the barn. I heard Sam greet you at the door, but when Andy announced it was time to make lasagna and I didn't hear you coming down the hall, I thought you went in the kitchen."

"Nope."

"I freaked you out, didn't I?"

"Yes, ma'am."

"Well, now that you've experienced the most thrilling and terrifying moment of a writer's life, catching someone reading your book, could you spare me ten or fifteen minutes of your time?"

"Are you serious? You've agreed to read my book! You can have my time, my manual labor, my hack for hard-boiled eggs — anything you need, including, but not limited to, a kidney."

Desiree's grin widened. "See, that's why you'll make a success of this. You write the way you talk. You have an authentic voice and readers adore that, especially the ones you're going after."

Stunned by Desiree's words, she just stared at her as the praise rolled around in her fried brain. *Success, authentic voice, readers adore that.*

"You look a little wobbly. Would you like to sit down?"

She managed to nod. Slipping through the gap between the couch and Andy's chair, she lowered herself carefully to the couch cushion. Sam followed and rested his head on her knee.

"Breathe."

She obeyed Desiree's command and gulped in air while she stroked Sam's head.

"I should have led up to that comment. You write so well that I kinda forgot you're not used to getting feedback. I don't know which is harder to hear, criticism or praise. Typically we believe the criticism and disbelieve the praise."

She nodded again, then silently vowed that would be her last nod. She didn't want to turn into a bobblehead.

"I urge you to believe what I've just said, though. I'm only a little way in and clearly I need to read the whole thing to make sure you have a grasp of structure, but I already know you have a terrific voice."

"Thank—" She cleared her throat. "Thank you."

"Thank *you* for trusting me with your book. I can already see why Lucky wanted me to read it. This week is a little full, but—"

"*Please* don't let it interfere with your schedule."

"Oh, I won't. Angie gets top billing this week, but she's extremely organized so I'm not overly concerned about the wedding. And I'm enjoying your book, so it's a welcome escape from any drama that crops up."

"Let me repeat, if you need me to do—"

"I'll let you know. I do have one suggestion, more of a marketing concept than an editorial thing. This will be a series, right?"

"Right."

"Do you have a series name in mind?"

"Sort of. Maybe The Odette Chronicles?"

"That's not bad, but you have this group of girls who call themselves *The Losers Club*. I think that's your series title."

A burst of fireworks went off in her head, a reliable signal that an idea worked. "Yes. Much better. It's obvious, but I didn't see it."

"That's why it's good to have another pair of eyes. I'm really excited about—"

"Hey, Mom, call the *Sentinel*!" Rance came striding down the hall, followed by Andy and Lucky. "I made lasagna in the kitchen and we didn't have to use the fire extinguisher!"

Sam left Oksana and trotted over to Rance, tail wagging, to share in whatever new thing was going on.

"Congratulations, son." Desiree closed the book and crossed her arms over it. "I knew you had it in you."

"He did a good job, Dez." Andy sent Rance a look of approval. "You're not nearly as incompetent as you think you are."

"Hey, that's right." Rance grinned. "I have the *Sentinel*'s columnist right here. Gonna right about me next week?"

"You want me to?"

"Sure. Let the ladies in town know I'm not only a handsome cuss, I'm learning to cook. Didn't you say that was a selling point?"

Lucky snorted. "I don't think *learning to cook* will play as well as *able to cook*."

"I disagree. *Learning to cook* indicates I'm teachable, willing to try new things, step out of my comfort zone. Very attractive qualities in a potential mate. You could work that concept into the column, Andy."

"Want me to include your phone number?"

"They know where to find me. That's another perk of bartending at the Buffalo." He glanced at Oksana. "Enough about me. Did you enjoy your barn tour?"

"I did."

"Lucky didn't say much about it, but he did mention you were impressed that it wasn't overly fragrant."

"And he told me about the family rotation to keep it sweet-smelling."

"That's a big factor," Desiree said. "But it's also a sign of healthy horses. Marsh keeps a close eye on them. It's helpful to have a vet in the family."

"Whatever the routine, they're absolutely beautiful. Koko takes my breath away."

"Do you ride?"

"I love it, rode my friends' horses when I was in high school, but I'm out of practice."

"We can fix that. I know you have classes to keep up with, but please let me know when you have time to go out. With so many of us, usually someone's looking for a riding buddy."

"That sounds lovely. Thank you." Significantly, Lucky didn't volunteer to be that someone.

Desiree's generous offer didn't fit her schedule, anyway. This visit was an outlier. An hour of basketball with Ella at the high school gym was doable, but driving out to the ranch required a much bigger chunk of time and gas money.

And yet... she longed to take that time, to feel the rush of the wind against her cheeks as she cantered across a spring meadow on one of those dazzling horses. One tantalizing day at Rowdy Ranch made her hungry for more.

What would it be like to live this way twenty-four-seven? Talk about an impossible dream.

"Are we eating in front of the fire again?" Andy surveyed the group. "If we are, we need to build it up."

"I'll handle that." Lucky walked to the hearth and moved the metal screen.

Holding the book against her chest, Desiree stood. "I promised to call Vanessa tonight and let her know what kind of weather we're expecting for the ceremony. See you guys at dinner. Oh, and Sam—"

"Needs to go out." Andy glanced at her as she walked toward their bedroom. "I'm on it."

"Thanks, my love." She whisked through the doorway.

"Hey, Andy, I'll take Sam," Rance said. "You sit and relax. Come on, pup." Patting his thigh, he started back down the hall.

"Thanks, son." He sank into his chair and glanced over at Oksana. "I see you retrieved your laptop. Did we interrupt your work session when we barreled in like a herd of elephants?"

"No. I was talking with Desiree."

His eyebrows lifted. Then he waited until the front door closed behind Rance and Sam. "About your book?"

"Yes."

Lucky whirled around, a log in one gloved hand. "She's already read some of it? Was that what she was holding just now?"

"It was and she's just getting started, but…." She couldn't keep the grin from breaking through. "She loves my voice."

"Hot damn." His smile took over his whole face. "I knew she would. I *knew* it."

"She told me writers tend to believe the criticism and disbelieve the praise. She's right. I'm having a tough time getting my head around what she said."

"Which was?" Lucky ignored the dying fire, his expression eager. "Tell me what she said. All of it."

"That I would be successful because I have an authentic voice that will appeal to the readers I'm going for."

Lucky's eyes glowed with excitement. "Yeah, you do."

"Wow." Andy looked impressed. "That's high praise."

"Like I said, I'm having trouble believing it."

"But you can. And you should." Andy continued to gaze at her as if she'd just sprouted wings. "She knows what she's talking about."

"That's for sure," Lucky said. "You can take that to the bank, literally." Then he paused, his gaze meeting hers. "Not that the money angle is important. I know how you feel about—"

"Exactly. I'm not in it to make money."

Andy blinked. "Why not, for heaven's sake?"

"I chased that goal once before, with basketball. Lucky knows the story. I'm not making that mistake again."

"Well, I don't know the story, but if Dez says you'll be a success, she's not just talking about a critical success. She means you should be able to earn a living."

"But how can she know that?"

"Um, well..." Andy exchanged a glance with Lucky. "When you put it that way, I guess she can't, not for sure. Anyway, it's great that she's enthusiastic about the book."

"It's fantastic, and now I'm itching to get back to the second one. How much time before dinner?"

"About an hour."

"Then I'd like to excuse myself and do some writing in my room until then."

"By all means."

"See you later." Tucking her laptop under her arm, she made her way back to the cozy space and used pillows to prop herself up on the bottom bunk. She clicked on the file with a shiver of anticipation. And there was Odette, impatiently waiting for her to continue the story.

_**25**_

Lucky watched her walk away, his heart full. He'd been right about her book and her potential. His mom had just confirmed it.

Oksana had no concept of how significant that was, how far-reaching it might be. Which was okay. The whole truth would blow her mind. One step at a time.

"How long have you been in love with her?" Andy's soft question carried the weight of his years of experience.

Lucky turned back to him. Yeah, you didn't try to argue with a man who saw straight into your soul. He laid down the log he'd been holding. "From the minute she walked in to apply for the job. I've been lying to myself ever since."

"How about her?"

"Poor woman is hooked on me, too. But she'll get over it."

Andy stared at him in disbelief. "Why are you saying that? Sounds to me like you should be jumping for joy."

"Afraid not. She'll be leaving town."

"Are you sure?"

"I'm sure. Her dream is to be a school counselor and evidently this district has a waiting list of educators wanting to land a job here."

"I guess I'm not surprised. That award put us on the map. But she seems invested in her writing. If you two are in love, she could switch horses and do that, instead. With your mother's help—"

"Mom would have to uncloak. I'm not sure she'd—"

"She will. We've already talked about it, once we figured out you're nuts about her."

"When was that?"

"This morning when you two were eating breakfast. I'm amazed Rance hasn't picked up on it."

"He's convinced I've lost interest in dating, period. I'm not doing all the things."

"Like?"

"Flowers, candy, dinner and dancing," No, he'd bought Oksana a reading chair. Dorky.

Andy smiled. "Yeah, that's Rance, all right. But back to you and Oksana. If she returns your feelings, I don't see a problem. Dez will reveal who she is and offer to be her mentor. She might not earn a living immediately, but—"

"With Mom's contacts, it won't take long."

"It won't, and until she does, she has the bookstore job. And she'll have you. Everyone lives happily ever after."

Except he wasn't good enough for her. Especially now. He knew better than to say so because this kind man would argue the point. Andy wouldn't understand the underlying issue, either.

So instead he hauled out Oksana's likely objection. "She won't want to switch horses. She's been burned before." He quickly explained the basketball fiasco and managed to end it as Rance came through the front door with Sam.

"I'll let your mother know about that wrinkle," Andy murmured.

"Thanks." He glanced down the hall where Rance was wiping Sam's paws with a towel. A year ago he might not have bothered. He was more mindful these days.

Yeah, he still believed a massive truck and a flashy horse would impress the ladies, but he was loyal and absolutely fearless. The woman who fell for Rance would have to put up with some quirks, but she'd get a white knight in the bargain.

"Can't wait to come warm myself by the fire!" Rance called out as he turned Sam loose. "I'd say it's colder than hell out there, but hell's supposed to be hot, so I got nuthin'."

"Whoops." Lucky turned back to the fire, which had been reduced to a bed of coals. He added some kindling and smaller logs as Sam showed up and flopped down on his bed near the hearth.

"I'm getting a bottle of cider!" Rance's voice drifted out from the kitchen. "Anybody want one?"

"Sure!" Lucky called out and Andy echoed him.

The fire was just getting going when Rance walked in with three bottles and a bag of pretzels. "Happy hour is served." Then he paused. "That's what you call building up the fire?"

"I got distracted."

"By what? Where's Oksana?"

"In her room."

"Did you tick her off? Because you acted a little weird after you came back from the barn. If you've made her mad—"

"She's not mad. She had work to do and she wanted to finish it before dinner."

"Andy? You were here. Is he telling the truth?"

"He's telling the truth."

"That's good." He gave Andy one of the ciders and set another one on the coffee table. "What was the distraction, then?"

So much for telling the truth. He snuck a glance at Andy.

Andy tipped his bottle in his direction. "We were talking about Oksana."

He gulped. Surely Andy wouldn't... and he didn't. He launched into a tall tale about how much Oksana was enjoying herself and how impractical it would be for her to come out more often, considering her location and her online classes.

"Yeah, she's really motivated to get that degree." Rance opened the pretzels and pushed the bag in Andy's direction. "Now that's what I call a fire, bro. Come get you some pretzels and a bottle of cider."

"Appreciate it." He dropped down on the couch next to Rance and twisted the cap off his cider. He was glad Rance had interrupted the discussion with Andy.

He shouldn't be surprised that Andy and his mom had picked up on his obsession with

Oksana. His mother's perceptive abilities were legendary. With Andy as her sidekick, she'd doubled her powers.

"Earth to Lucky. Come in, Lucky." Rance nudged him.

"Sorry. Did you say something to me?"

"Andy and I've been talking about the plan for tomorrow. He's going into the office and could take you and Oksana to the bookshop, but if you don't have power by then—"

"That's the thing. There's no point in going back to the shop unless the line's been repaired. I've heard nothing so far. Are you working at the Buffalo tomorrow?"

"Clint scheduled me to start at noon, so depending on what the electric company has to say, I could take you in when I go. We'll leave a little early so I can help with your truck."

"Let's plan on that. Gives more time for the power line to be fixed. Thanks."

"I have barn duty in the morning. Care to help me?"

He chuckled. "Saw that coming."

"If I hadn't asked, you'd think something was wrong with me."

"So true."

"Hey, Andy." Rance took another handful of pretzels. "How're the wedding plans coming along?"

"Just fine, I hope, since we're only three days away."

"Not that wedding. Your wedding."

"Oh, *that* wedding."

"Yeah, *that* wedding. It's been weeks since Mom proposed. When are you two going to tie the knot?"

"We couldn't very well set something up before Angie had hers. That wouldn't be right."

"But you could still pick a date for some time after Angie's married off. If you have set one, I haven't heard about it. Lucky, have you heard anything?"

"Nope." Having the spotlight on Andy instead of him was nice for a change.

"Well, she has a deadline coming up."

Rance snorted. "She always has a deadline coming up. If you wait until she doesn't have a deadline, you'll be old and gray before you walk down that aisle."

"I'm already gray."

"My point exactly! It's not like you have sixty years ahead of you. Push her, Andy. I'd tell you to kidnap her and take her to Vegas but then we'd all miss out."

"Yeah, don't do that." Lucky jumped in. "Everyone has to be there. All of us, the Wenches, I'm thinking of other folks, too, people she's known for more than thirty years."

Andy's eyes widened. "Are we talking about an extravaganza?"

"Yes!" Rance pointed the tip of his bottle at him. "And *you* have to start the ball rolling because chances are she won't. She'll let the engagement drag on forever."

"He's right," Lucky said. "She's never been married or even engaged. You need to take the reins, here."

"What if she doesn't want to make a big deal out of it?"

Rance gazed at him. "I don't think she has a choice."

<u>26</u>

Oksana participated in the dinner conversation, but her attention kept shifting to Desiree and replaying what she'd said about the book. Had she really used the word *success*? What did that mean?

Examined closely, it was a vague word. Everyone measured success differently. She could end up with a few dedicated readers. If the series helped them through the difficult pre-teen and teen years, that was a form of success.

But the more kids she helped, the better, right? She didn't care about the money, so maybe she'd price it low to encourage more people to buy it.

Or she could give it away! Why not? Then anybody could have it. In that case she wouldn't need a publisher. An editor, definitely. Maybe she could pay Desiree to do it. Or Andy, who actually was one. He might help her find a printer and maybe knew a way to distribute the book.

Desiree and Andy's knowledge would be valuable if she decided to go that route and no telling when she'd get another opportunity to ask these questions.

But Rance was at the table. Then again, why not tell him? Lucky had said he could be trusted not to spill the beans.

She waited for a lull in the conversation. Then she looked at Desiree, who sat at the end of the long table, with Andy and Rance to her left and Lucky and Oksana to her right. "I've decided to tell Rance about my book."

She looked startled but quickly composed herself. "Okay."

"*Book?*" Rance's fork clattered to his plate. "You wrote one?"

"Your mom's critiquing it."

"No shit." Then he blinked. "Sorry, Mom."

She smiled. "It's okay, son. She figured out I'm probably qualified after all the years the Wenches and I have been reviewing them."

He studied his mother. "The Wenches. Of course. That makes sense." Then he turned back to Oksana. "What's it about?"

"A fictional girl going through the years between eleven and fifteen. It'll be a series. Lucky's read most of it."

"Whoa!" He reared back. "Way to keep a secret, dude."

"I promised."

Rance nodded. "I get it. Andy, did you know about this?"

"I told him," Desiree said. "I warned Oksana that I have no secrets from Andy, but I promised not to mention the book to anyone else, including anyone in the family."

"That puts me in a special group, then. You can trust me, Oksana. I won't squeal."

"That's what Lucky said."

"Thanks for that, bro." He gave Lucky a thumbs-up before switching his focus to her. "I have a question, though. Why tell me?"

"I want to discuss an idea I had about the project and this is a golden opportunity. No telling how soon I'll get another one like it."

"Alrighty, then. Discuss away. I'm a vault."

"Okay." She took a breath. "First of all, Lucky was enthusiastic about the book and so far, Desiree is, too. That's encouraging. I might have something that others will want to read. Once it's edited, of course."

"Everyone needs editing," Lucky said, "but I didn't find a whole lot you'll need to fix in the part I read."

"That's good to hear. Anyway, my goal is to help kids through a difficult time in their lives, and I don't care if I make money or not, so instead of trying to land a publisher, why not self-publish and give it away for free? It seems like I'd reach more readers that way."

Silence. The old cliché was true. She could have heard a pin drop.

Then Desiree tucked her napkin beside her plate and pushed back her chair. "Keep eating, everybody, while I have a chat with Oksana." She glanced over, her gaze gentle and her smile kind. "Come with me."

"All right." Heart pounding, she left the table and followed Desiree through the living room. Behind her, the clink of utensils meant the guys had gone back to their meal, but they remained ominously quiet. "Did I say something wrong?"

"No, sweetheart. You just don't have all the facts, and I'm the only one who can give them to you. I wasn't planning to say anything yet, but it's time you learn who I am."

"Who you are? Are you like an international spy or something?"

She laughed. "Nothing that exciting." She headed for the library. "But I do have another name."

"Would I recognize it?"

"Yes."

"I can't imagine who it would be. Amelia Earhart would be a hundred and twenty-something by now."

"I'm not as famous as Amelia." She walked quickly through the library and pushed on one of the shelves.

Oksana gasped. "A revolving bookcase!"

"It adds drama to what I'm about to show you. I do relish a little drama." She stepped through the opening and stood aside to let Oksana come in. "Welcome to the office of M.R. Morrison. Which is me. That's my other name."

Her mouth dropped open. The huge curved desk covered with scattered notes, the keyboard, the large monitor, the bookshelves lining the walls, picture windows with a view of the Sapphires — it all looked like the office of a bestselling author.

Then she peered at the spines of those books and discovered multiple editions of each title, including foreign ones. Finally her attention swung back to Desiree. "Did he die? Are you his daughter?"

"Interesting. You're the first person who's come to that conclusion. The truth is, I made him up. I gave him John Wayne's real name, except I opted for M.R. instead of Marion Robert. Most people don't get the reference."

"I didn't. So all this time...." Still processing the news, she scanned the bookshelves again. "Why?"

"Thirty years ago most readers wouldn't pick up a Western written by a woman. My agent and publisher insisted on it. We created a reclusive old guy who hated having his picture taken."

"But you raised a bunch of kids in a small town! How in the heck did you keep it a secret for so many years?"

"The kids were trained at a very young age to maintain strict silence about Mommy's job. Most folks don't know any bestselling authors personally, so it never occurred to them that I was one. According to the grapevine, I inherited a grubstake and invested well."

"That was one of my versions."

"It's partly true. When writers start making money they need to invest. Then you're not at the mercy of the market."

"Obviously you've done well."

"I've been fortunate. I've connected with readers who are eager for books I love writing. But I started small and built my readership gradually."

"You didn't have to tell me this. You could have critiqued my book, let me self-publish it and give it away."

"No, I couldn't. Not in good conscience. You could make a living as a writer without my connections, but with them you'll likely get there faster."

"You'd do that for me?"

"I would love to. Cloaking myself robbed me of that joy. I've never been able to help a promising talent make a go of it. Then, against all odds, here you are. But if counseling is your dream job, I won't mess with that."

"I... I... it's a bit overwhelm—"

"You don't have to decide right this minute. I know about the basketball disaster. Take your time. I'm not going anywhere and neither are you."

Emotion crowded her chest, making it hard to breathe. "I've wanted to meet you for years so I could tell you how much I love your books. I do. I'm crazy about them."

"Thank you. I have a hunch I'll be crazy about yours, too. Let's go finish dinner."

27

Lucky had a fair idea how the conversation had gone between his mom and Oksana. Neither of them chose to discuss it when they returned. Oksana looked shell-shocked, which was a typical reaction when someone outside the family learned his mother's identity.

In Oksana's case, the news had wider implications. Potentially life-changing ones. But she made no attempt to get him alone to discuss the matter.

Just as well. He couldn't predict the outcome and he sure as hell didn't want to influence it. When Rance suggested a pool tournament among the five of them, his mom and Oksana bowed out.

After giving Andy a shellacking that he took in his typical good-humored way, Lucky and Rance strolled down the hallway of the kids' wing on their way to bed. The faint click of computer keys drifted from under Oksana's door as they passed by.

Rance grinned. "She likes the old typewriter sound."

"Whatdya mean?"

"Computer keys usually don't make that much noise on their own. But on some laptops, you can change that in settings."

"Huh. Didn't know that."

"Mom used to stay up late and type. Keyboards were noisier then. I'd hear her when I went to get a drink of water."

"For all we know she still types late into the night. We're just not around to keep track."

Rance lowered his voice. "Any idea what Oksana's gonna do?"

"Nope."

"Seems like a no-brainer to me, but we've had the benefit of watching Mom work this program." Walking into the bedroom they'd moved out of seven years ago, he flipped a switch. The lamp on the nightstand between the twin beds came on.

The base was a replica of a Conestoga wagon and he'd adored it when he was younger. Still did, in fact. "It's surprising one of us hasn't written a book. You know, followed in her footsteps."

"They're mighty big footsteps." Rance sat on the bed by the window, the one he'd claimed when they'd lost possession of the bunks to Angie. He pulled off his boots. "When did Oksana give you her book?"

"Last night." He tossed his pillow on a chair and put on the bottom sheet he'd pulled from the linen closet earlier.

"If you finished a good chunk of it, you must have stayed up reading."

"I did. It's that good." Grabbing a pillowcase, he slipped it on.

"I'm kinda glad she's not writing Westerns."

"Why?"

"Just seems like if someone's going to carry on Mom's legacy, it should be one of us."

"Well, I don't see anybody stepping up to the plate."

"Because it would be damned intimidating. Like following Babe Ruth in the batting order." He took off his jeans and crawled into bed, stretching out on the mattress pad and pulling a quilt over him. "Honestly, a bottom sheet *and* a top sheet? You're such a dork."

Lucky grinned. "And you're such a barbarian." They hadn't traded that insult in years.

"I'd forgotten how much I like that old lamp."

"Yeah, me, too." He got out of his clothes, climbed into bed and pulled the small chain that turned off the lamp.

"Remember when we were wrestling and knocked it on the floor?"

"Made me sick to my stomach when the wheel broke off."

"But we glued it on again and you'd never know."

"Did you tell?"

"No. Did you?"

"No."

"Then let's keep it that way." Rance sighed. "I like being back in this house, just for a night. I appreciate things in a way I didn't when I lived here. Know what I mean?"

"Yeah." But he didn't. Not really. He'd always appreciated everything, always been aware that his presence hadn't been a done deal like Rance's. He'd just been lucky. And he was reminded of it every time someone said his name.

* * *

The electric company didn't contact him until nine-thirty. They'd traced the problem to a downed tree branch and expected to have power restored within the hour.

A bright sun was quickly transforming the landscape as he rode to town in the back seat of Rance's truck. The bedroll, washed and dried during the time he'd spent in his cabin yesterday, sat beside him. Oksana didn't talk much and neither did he, although he'd bet their thoughts were focused on the same unspoken topic.

Hard-packed snow had turned to slush that kept up a steady hiss under the truck's oversized tires. Rance bridged gaps in the conversation with speculation about what the Armstrong family would think of Wagon Train.

"I'm glad the snow's melting." He slowed as he reached the edge of town. "But it doesn't look very pretty. We show off best after a light, gentle snow that leaves picturesque drifts on the windowpanes." He sighed. "Like I said, Angie should have picked May. May is nice for a wedding."

"She was never going to pick May, bro."

"So true, but you know what? Andy and Mom could. Let's mount a campaign for them to get married in May."

"They haven't set a date?" Oksana looked surprised. "After all the hullabaloo on New Year's Eve?"

"They have not." Rance cruised down Main Street, where business owners were out with shovels clearing the sidewalk. "Andy used this wedding as their excuse for holding off, but they could have picked any time after that. Then he mentioned Mom's deadline as another hurdle."

"When is that?" Didn't sound like an idle question. She was leading up to something.

"May first, I think. Lucky? Do you remember?"

"That sounds right. I don't keep as close track as I did when we lived at home."

"Do you know how she's coming along on the book?" Another question with a slight edge to it.

"I don't have that info," Rance said. "Again, we were better informed when we lived there. Had to be. You didn't make stupid requests when she was getting close, especially if she was behind."

Oksana sighed. "I *really* don't want my book to interfere with her writing. That would be awful."

"It won't." Lucky hurried to calm that fear. "She wouldn't have agreed if she'd been worried about it."

"If you say so." But she still had a little crease between her eyebrows.

Rance pulled up in front of the bookshop. "Looks like I won't have to help you dig out your truck, bro. Just let it sit there and you'll be good to go by five tonight, no problem."

"Should be. Thanks for the ride."

"Yes, thanks." Oksana laid a hand on his arm. "I don't know what we would have done without you. You and Midnight Thunder."

He shrugged. "Freeze to death, most likely."

"Hey, I would *not* have let her freeze to death. I would have burned the furniture before I'd let that happen."

"Well, I'm glad we didn't have to resort to burning the furniture." She glanced back at him, a glint of amusement in her dark eyes.

Was she thinking about the broken bed? Even if she wasn't, now he was. And the mattress on the floor upstairs....

His phone pinged with a text. "Looks like we've got power." He opened his door and grabbed the bedroll. "Oksana, I'll get you—"

"No worries." She opened her door, stepped out carefully and reached for her duffel on the floor. "It's not bad right here. I have my key." She fished it out of her coat pocket. "I'll open up." She closed the truck door and started making her way through the melting snow.

Rance gazed after her. "You know, if she goes for this writing thing, she won't have to leave town."

"That's right."

"I never considered asking her out because I knew she wouldn't be staying, but if she does stay...."

The low protest deep in his throat just happened. Couldn't stop it. Couldn't cover it with a cough.

Rance scooted around in the seat and looked him in the eye. "I'll be damned. How long has this been going on?"

"Nothing's going on."

"The hell it's not. You warned me off just now. Which is fine. If that's how it is, I'll—"

"That's not how it is and if she stays, you should ask her out."

"I can't believe I didn't see it. You're in love with her. That's what the red chair was all about. That's why you stayed up all night reading her book and took a big chance asking Mom to read it."

"So what? I'm not the right guy for her."

"Who says?"

"I do! Drop it, bro. I need to get in there. Thanks for the ride." Jumping down without looking, he splashed into a puddle and sent icy water flying up, soaking his jeans, specifically his fly. Lovely.

<u>28</u>

To Oksana's surprise, customers had shown up soon after she'd turned the sign on the door to OPEN. They'd continued in a steady stream.

Some had claimed they'd been caught flat-footed by the blizzard and weren't going to let *that* happen again. Others had said they'd spent their forced confinement reading and needed to restock. A third group was shopping in advance since the bookstore would be closed on Wednesday for the wedding.

She and Lucky had barely managed to eat the sandwiches they'd made before leaving the ranch this morning. She'd only been upstairs once, to fetch her hairdryer so he could get rid of the wet spot on his fly.

She'd avoided looking at the mattress on the floor. He'd wisely gone into the storeroom to dry his jeans and she'd wisely not followed him there.

He'd clearly decided to keep his distance, especially during the rare moments they'd been alone in the shop. But every so often she'd turned, her gaze colliding with his, and the air had crackled.

She'd been aware of him every minute of the day, her senses recording his movements — reshelving books, schmoozing with customers, laughing with some high school boys who'd stopped by after school in search of brownies.

When she'd explained about the power outage, they'd gone across the street to the Buffalo and brought her a big slice of chocolate cake. It was still in its to-go box on the counter, untouched.

At closing time they were down to one customer, and she wanted to chat. Oksana made polite conversation while Lucky reconciled the day's receipts. She gradually maneuvered the woman toward the front of the shop and was finally able to usher her out the door.

Closing and locking it, she flipped the sign over with a sigh of relief. "Evidently blizzards inspire people to read print books."

"Sure. Even if folks still have power, they might lose Wi-Fi. Several people said that happened, and that's when they turned to their print books." He closed the cash drawer. "That does it for today. I'd hoped to get to the dump, but it's closed."

She moved slowly back toward the cash wrap, heart thumping. Would he just leave? "There's always tomorrow."

"Yeah, but I'd like to get it out of the storeroom. You were right. It's tough to move around in there." His gaze was hard to read.

"Would you really have burned the furniture?"

"Damn straight. I would have started with those slats, which are actual wood. You can't burn particle board, though. And books... well, that would have been a last resort."

"I couldn't have let you burn books." She stepped closer, drawn to him by an invisible string. "Not even to save me."

"Sorry, but I wouldn't have let you stand in my way. You're more precious than all the books in this shop." He said it casually.

But she caught the flicker of heat in his eyes. Tendrils of arousal curled through her body. They had an agreement. If she reminded him of it, he'd grab his coat and walk out the door. "Those boys were sweet to bring me cake."

"They all have a huge crush on you."

"They do?"

"You can't tell? They say they're here for the brownies, but you're the draw." The flicker became a soft glow.

"What makes you think that?"

"I was seventeen once. I recognize the signs." He nudged the to-go box in her direction. "Don't forget to take it upstairs. It won't improve with age."

Upstairs. Hearing him say the word made her quiver with longing.

He sucked in a breath. "I should go."

"Don't."

With a groan, he reached for her, pulling her close, capturing her mouth with a kiss that made her dizzy, pulling her blouse from the waistband of her jeans.

She fumbled with the snaps of his shirt.

He lifted his head, gasping. "I shouldn't be—"

"No one has to know."

"Oksana...."

"Make love to me. Please."

"You drive me crazy." Cupping her tush, he lifted her up and headed for the stairs.

"Wait. I'm too heavy." But she couldn't resist wrapping her legs around him and feeling the jut of his cock between her thighs.

"You're lighter than that chair." But he was puffing by the time they reached the landing.

"Put me down so I can get the door."

When he did, she flung it open, reached for his hand and yanked him across the threshold.

He stumbled in, his laughter breathless. "Somebody's serious about this."

"Dead serious." She toed off her boots while unbuttoning her blouse. She was breathing hard and she hadn't made that climb. "You know where the condoms are."

"Yes, ma'am. Aye, aye, ma'am."

She was down to her underwear by the time he came back and tossed the foil package on the mattress. She reached for the back hooks of her bra.

"Hang on. I want to take that off."

She paused. "It's not the fancy kind."

"No." Chest heaving, he closed the gap between them and slid both hands behind her back. "It's like the ones that were hanging on the dryer rack when I first came in here. I have a fondness for those."

He gently unhooked the bra, drew it away and stepped back. It fell to the floor as he looked at her as if memorizing... everything. Swallowing, he met her gaze. "Thank you for letting me love you."

Her heartbeat quickened at his choice of words. He hadn't said *make love to you.* Did that mean he was ready to claim the joy they'd found? To speak it out loud?

Before she could come up with a response, he was back, kissing her face, her throat, her breasts. Scooping her up, he laid her on the mattress and followed her down, stripping away her panties, continuing his sweet assault.

He didn't miss an inch of skin that was within reach. Then he gave her the most intimate kiss of all. He took his time, seemingly in no rush to make her come.

His slow, languorous approach had the opposite effect. Her eager body welcomed the onslaught, rising to the occasion with a climax that spun her around like a carnival ride. She laughed. She screeched. She called his name. Over and over and over.

As her breathing slowed, he kissed her damp thighs. "Be with you soon."

She watched him undress, this man she loved. And he loved her. She knew it. What idiot wouldn't grab him with both hands?

Thanks to Desiree, aka M.R. Morrison, she could. She'd always loved writing more than studying. Was she taking a risk? Yes. So worth it.

When he moved over her, the intensity in his green eyes took her breath away. That was love, all right, a forever, 'til death do us part kind of love. Holding her gaze, he thrust deep.

Yes. This was what she wanted — years and years with Lucky McLintock. It was all so clear. Nothing left except to tell him.

But first... ahhh, he knew just what to do, how to make her body melt into his, how to warm her from head to toe with the love shining in his eyes.

His pace quickened, his gaze still locked with hers. He didn't speak, didn't ask if she was close.

Because he knew. Her heart swelled. He knew her in a way no one ever had. Which left her free to abandon herself to the pleasure he gave her. With a cry of joy, she surrendered to the wonder of coming apart in his arms.

The ecstasy of it doubled when he came, too. And he called her name. For the first time, he called her name.

The sweet sound of it echoed in her head as she lay beneath him, his forehead resting on her shoulder, his breath coming in shuddering gasps. She stroked his back and planned what she would say and how she would say it.

He lifted his head. "I have to—"

"I know. Hurry back. We need to talk."

After he left, she sat up and turned on the electric stove beside the bed. This was cozy. She might leave it this way, at least for a while, until she moved into — whoa, better slow the heck down.

She untucked the blanket so she could wrap up in it. She left a section for him.

Except when he came back, he pulled on his briefs and his socks. Then he reached for his jeans and put those on, too.

"You're getting dressed?"

"I can't stay. Rance is working a double shift at the Buffalo. He'll notice if my truck's still parked out front."

"Maybe it doesn't matter anymore."

He gave her a long look. "Why not?"

She patted the mattress. "Come sit. I have something to tell you."

"Okay." He looked wary, but he lowered himself to the mattress.

Couldn't he guess what she was about to say? Shouldn't he be smiling? He'd sat beside her, so she scooted around to face him, so she could see him better. "It'll be no surprise to you that your mother offered to give me a leg up the publishing ladder and encouraged me to consider writing as a career instead of counseling."

He nodded. "Figured she would."

"I had to think about it. I've put a lot of time and money into my education."

"I know."

"But like you said about pool and bookselling, I *like* the study of child psychology and I *love* writing fiction. Besides, everything I've learned will enrich what I write, so it's not like I wasted that time and money."

"That's great to hear." The light was back in his eyes. "I hoped you'd see it that way. Have you contacted Mom? Does she know? Because she'll be thrilled."

"I haven't contacted her, but I will."

"You could text her tonight. This is news that shouldn't wait." He started to get up.

"I'm not finished."

"You're not?" The wary look returned but he sank down again.

"Don't look so worried. I'm not going to quit. I need this job until I start making money. I might have to go parttime eventually, but I love working here almost as much as writing, which is saying a lot."

"I'll be glad to have you."

"Would you care to expand on that?"

He frowned. "What do you mean?"

"Good grief, don't you see? I'll be staying! You're one of the reasons I made that decision!"

The color drained from his face. "Don't say that. I can't be the—"

"Not *the* reason. That would put too much pressure on this brand-new thing we have going on. But I won't lie. You... us... that was a big factor."

He dragged in a breath. "Oksana, what happened just now... I was planning to tell you it won't ever—"

"Are you dumping me?"

"No! I just—"

"You love me, dammit! Tell me I'm wrong."

Despair darkened his gaze. "I have no right."

"No *right*? What the hell, Lucky. You're the complete package — honorable, kind, intelligent, sexy as sin, and part of a wonderful family."

"No, I'm not."

"Not what? I dare you to disprove—"

"I told you. Becoming part of that family was the luck of the—"

"And it's a heartwarming story. You should be—"

"Grateful?" He got up. "I am, every day. But the ugly truth is I'm the son of a man with no morals and a woman who didn't give a damn about me."

"Who cares? I certainly don't."

"You should." Grabbing his shirt off the floor, he shoved his arms into the sleeves. "Especially if you want kids. What if—"

"That's ridiculous. Things can happen even when—"

"Rance told me he's interested."

"You're pawning me off on your *brother*?"

"He's a great guy."

"And you're an idiot!" If she'd had something to throw at him, she would have let it fly.

"No question about that." Picking up his boots, he charged out the door and thundered down the stairs.

She would have followed to yell at him some more and maybe find something to throw when he paused to put on his boots and coat.

But she was naked and the lights were still on in the shop. Instead she jumped up and down on the mattress, shouting insults at the top of her lungs. Maybe later she'd cry, but not now.

She was too damn mad for tears.

29

Right after Lucky walked into his dark cabin, his cell rang. His mother. "Hey, Mom."

"What's going on?"

"What do you mean?"

"I just got off the phone with Oksana. Did you tell her she'd be better off with your brother?"

He closed his eyes and muttered a swear word.

"What was that?"

"Nothing. I just... I might have said something to that effect." If only he hadn't made that parting comment. He truly was an idiot.

"Why the hell would you say a thing like that, son? You love her!"

"That's why I said it. She hasn't thought this through, but I have. I'm not the one for her."

"Well, she thinks you are, or she did, before you made that bonehead suggestion. Now she's spitting nails, and I can't say I blame her."

"What else did she say?"

"Oh, we started off just fine. She'd texted me her decision, which made me very happy, so I called her. Naturally I asked if she'd told you and how you'd reacted. That's when she went sort of weird on me, talking all around the subject."

His heart ached. She'd tried to protect him.

"So I pushed a little bit."

"Mm." He was in *big* trouble.

"When I asked point blank if that meant you two would be socializing more, she told me you'd recommended your brother, instead."

"It was just an idea. They get along, so I—"

"Let's cut to the chase. Why are you rejecting this lovely woman who's crazy about you?"

"She could do better."

"If you keep up this nonsense I'm inclined to agree. But that's too vague. What do you think's wrong with you?"

He took a deep breath. "It's not so much me as where I came from."

"Wagon Train?"

"No, the people I... my... biological parents."

The heavy silence on the other end didn't bode well.

"Don't get me wrong. I'm extremely grateful to you for giving me a wonderful home and a loving family, but—"

"Tell you what. It's now... six-thirty. Be over here at seven-thirty."

"For what?"

"You'll find out when you get here. You might want to eat something before you come. I won't be serving snacks."

He'd heard that tone a few times in his life. When she had that edge of steel in her voice, the best course of action was to do what she asked. "I'll be there."

* * *

He didn't eat. The way his stomach was jumping around, it wouldn't have tolerated food. His suspicion that she'd used the hour to call a family meeting was verified when he saw the trucks lined up in the parking area.

Even Midnight Thunder was there, and Rance was supposed to be working at the Buffalo tonight. Had she put out a Code Red? Just because of his stupid-ass comment about Oksana dating Rance? That was a little extreme.

Sam greeted him at the door as always, but his mother did not. The sound of voices in an animated discussion came from the living room. Was that Angie carrying on about something? She was supposed to be resting up for her big day.

He walked in to discover a blazing fire and a select group gathered nearby. Chairs had been added to the semi-circle, which had been pushed back from the hearth, probably to give him room to stand there and be roasted.

But nobody was sitting down yet. Instead they'd formed a loose circle with everyone talking at once.

"He's here," his mother announced. "The McLintock family meeting is now in session. You can all take your seats. Except Lucky."

He glanced at the group of ten. "But this isn't everybody."

"It's everybody who's directly connected to this matter, *son*. And if you're wondering if I deliberately emphasized that word, I absolutely did. This is your family, the core members who've lived with you in this house."

He took his place beside the fire. Standing in front of it might be symbolic but he was already sweating through his shirt. "I have to apologize. I made a lame comment, almost a joke, to Oksana earlier tonight and I shouldn't have. It was uncalled for. I'll apologize to her as soon as I have the opportunity."

Sky threw out the first question. "What'd you say?"

"I suggested she'd be better off with Rance instead of me."

"*What?*" Rance came out of his chair. "Did she clock you? I hope she did, because if she didn't—"

"Sit down, Rance." His mother motioned him back to his seat. "I want Lucky to tell us why he said it."

His chest tightened as he scanned the beloved faces in front of him. They'd arranged themselves in birth order, the way they rode when they went out on the trail as a family—His mom, Sky, Beau, Clint, Cheyenne, Marsh, Bret, Gil, Rance and Angie.

"I love you all." His throat hurt and he cleared it. "I love this family. I'm the luckiest guy here, which is why my name fits. I'm also the only one here because of luck. The rest of you were planned for, anticipated."

"Not me," Sky said. "Totally unplanned."

"I stand corrected. But you know who your dad was. You know he was a good guy. All of you know that. Except me."

Beau nodded. "I used to think I had a horrible dad. Messed with my mind for a long time. I can see how this could trip you up."

"I'm glad this is out in the open, bro," Marsh said. "Since you never talked about it, I think we all figured it was old news."

"And those unknown people." Angie gazed at him, her blue eyes warm with affection. "Do they even matter when you have so many known people in your family? Doesn't that make up for it?"

"It does, in a way. Usually I can forget about how I came to be born. But sometimes I... can't. Then I say stupid stuff like I did to Oksana."

"But you'll patch it up, right?" Bret, ever the optimist, gave him a smile. "We've all had to dig ourselves out of a hole at some point. Well, not Rance, but he'll get his turn to screw up a promising relationship."

And there was the sticking point. He would try to smooth things over with Oksana, but instead he'd likely make things worse, since he believed what he'd told her. She could do better.

He'd believed that from the beginning, when their relationship had been billed as temporary. But the scenario had shifted, largely due to his own actions and now their working relationship was in shambles.

Nice work, doofus. He might have connected her to his mom, but he'd ruined the job she loved almost as much as writing. Could he repair that damage? Didn't look promising.

Gil's eyebrows lifted. "That long silence is telling. I'll take a wild guess you're not going to patch things up."

"The truth is, I've made some very bad decisions lately and I'll pay dearly for them. I'm hoping Oksana and I can get along as friends and co-workers, but—"

"Friends and co-workers my ass." Rance stood. "Are you still saying you're not good enough for her?"

"Because I'm not, okay?" The tightness in his chest got worse. "I love everyone in this room more than I can ever say." He started to choke up. "But I'm not like you." Time to leave. "I'm not a McLintock." He made a break for it and got out the door before anyone came after him.

Eyes blurry with what he refused to admit were tears, he hopped in his truck and drove like a bat out of hell back to his cabin, spewing mud and slush like he was in some monster truck rally.

The roar of an F-350 behind him told him it was either his mother or Rance. When he slammed on the brakes in the parking area beside his porch, Midnight Thunder skidded to a stop right behind him with no more than an inch of clearance.

Rance leaped out, leaving the motor running. "I should whip your sorry ass!"

"Go ahead if it'll make you feel any better."

"How could you say that? How could you say you're not a McLintock?" Rance gulped for air. "Did you see how we all showed up? Did you see that?"

"I'm sorry everyone was inconvenienced. Nobody needed to—"

"Yes, we did, and you wanna know why? Because Mom said you needed us! We came because you needed us, Lucky, and then you…you…" He gulped again and swiped at his nose with the sleeve of his coat.

"Like I said, I'm sorry. Really sorry."

Rance sniffed. "You meant the world to me, you bastard." His voice was clogged with emotion. "Because of you, I always had a buddy, someone m-my age." He sniffed again.

Dear God, he was crying. He hadn't seen Rance cry since they were six.

"We were a team, you and m-me. I could be the screw-up b-because you were always there to keep m-me from k-killing myself."

"You weren't always a—"

"And you know who we were? We were the McLintock brothers, damn it! And now you say you're not? Well, fuck you!" Whirling around, he leaped back in his truck, slammed the door and backed out going way too fast.

Lucky waited for the crunch. He'd hit a tree, sure as the world. By some miracle he didn't.

Rance was the only member of the family who contacted him, which left the rest of a very long night to contemplate what his brother had said. He used every single minute of that night.

30

On one hand, Oksana was relieved when Lucky texted that he wouldn't be in. On the other hand, she cursed him for being a coward. If she could show up, why couldn't he?

Even more maddening, when she looked in the storeroom, every piece of the broken bed was gone. He'd come like a thief in the night. A later text, though, made her glad he'd taken away the evidence of their wild night. He was sending her two helpers from the Wenches, Annette and Colleen.

Like all members of the book club, they were regulars so they knew the place well. They turned out to be awesome saleswomen, too. Customers got a kick out of finding two women from the town's elite book club filling in for Lucky. Browsers turned into buyers.

The pair even seemed to know when a customer would respond to the quiet, intellectual approach that was Annette's specialty and when they'd prefer Colleen's bubbly personality. During a break Oksana asked them how they worked that program.

"You look for clues," Annette said. "How they dress, how they wear their hair."

"Guys are a little tougher." Colleen straightened the hem of her red sweater dotted with jeweled hearts. "They don't carry purses. You can tell so much from a woman's purse."

"We're a perfect example of giving out clues." Annette swept a hand over her conservative indigo blouse and gray slacks. "When we organized years ago, we each chose our color. I went straight for a muted one."

"While I grabbed red."

"That would've been my choice, too." Oksana had put on a favorite red shirt since Valentine's Day was hours away. So was the wedding. And seeing Lucky again.

"I've noticed you wear a lot of it. I've loved that color since childhood. Nancy wanted it, too, so we had to draw straws. She's much happier with yellow now that she's added gold to the mix."

"And everyone else got the color they wanted?"

"They did." Annette smiled. "No more arguments. I hate arguments."

"Civilized debates, Annette. That's what we have. Thank goodness Teresa wanted orange. She's the only one with the complexion for it. She complains during Christmas because she clashes with everything, but in the fall she's a happy camper."

"There wasn't a battle for purple?"

"As if," Annette said with a chuckle.

"Yeah, right." Colleen laughed, too. "Desiree's the head honcho. She got first pick. She chose well. The color of royalty suits her."

"Yes, it does." Oksana hugged her secret close. These two didn't know about her book or that she'd been brought into the fold. Someday soon she'd tell Desiree she was free to explain everything to the Wenches.

Her confidence in her writing had risen exponentially since Sunday night. But after last night's disaster, her confidence in being able to work with Lucky was in the cellar. What did it say about the situation that he couldn't face her today?

At five on the dot, she thanked Colleen and Annette for giving L'Amour and More their valuable time.

"I had a blast," Colleen said. "Tell Lucky I'm happy to fill in whenever he needs me."

"Same here." Annette pulled on a sleek indigo trench coat. "This was fun."

"I'll let him know." As they left, a light bulb flashed in her brain. Would they like a parttime job? Adding two enthusiastic, knowledgeable employees would allow Lucky to work on the expansion project without worrying about keeping sales elevated at this location.

But would he slay his demons and talk to his mother about his ideas? If only he could realize he was his own worst enemy.

She locked the door, flipped over the sign and located the special one she'd created for tomorrow. As she propped it in the window, she glanced across the street. A row of familiar trucks sat diagonally parked in front of the Buffalo.

The wedding rehearsal at the church must be over. The rehearsal dinner had begun. The McLintocks had gathered.

She gazed at the door as it opened and closed. When she figured out she was hoping to see Lucky, she turned away.

Damn his hide. She alternated between wanting to slap him and longing to hold him until she somehow chased the bad dreams away.

Totally unrealistic. She was a psychology major, for God's sake. She couldn't fix Lucky's problems. He had to do it. And if he couldn't, then he was lost to her.

She still hadn't cried. Maybe she never would. Maybe she'd just tolerate this frustration and despair until she finally worked through it.

Turning off the lights, she climbed the stairs. She needed to steam the wrinkles out of her red dress. She would wear it, not for Lucky McLintock, but for herself. And just a tiny bit to show him what he'd given up.

She flicked on the wall switch when she stepped into her apartment and glanced over at the red chair. He'd been so excited to get it here, so funny about bringing up the ottoman right away so he could see how the combo looked in her apartment.

Oh, the light in his eyes when she'd raved about that chair. And his sweet grin.

Then the tears came.

* * *

Across the street, Lucky stood in the shadows waiting for the lights to go out in the bookshop. Collar turned up against the cold, he watched hungrily as Oksana moved through the familiar closing ritual, walking quickly, ponytail swinging. He cursed the hearts and Cupids which partly blocked his view.

Things had gone well with Colleen and Annette. He could tell from everyone's body language as she'd bid them goodbye. They'd been good sports to agree at the last minute.

He'd been prepared to go through the list until he found at least one who could do it. No way would he have left Oksana alone, today of all days. She could handle it, but she shouldn't have to.

Colleen had said yes immediately and had suggested pairing up with Annette, a yin and yang thing. After the wedding, he'd come up with a way to thank them for being such troupers.

As for Oksana... would she ever forgive him? He ached for her. The visceral pain had been with him ever since he'd left the night before.

When he'd driven in the back way at dawn and let himself in through the storeroom door, he'd vowed to work silently, a huge undertaking considering what he'd had to load. He'd cushioned the metal truck bed with old blankets and lowered each section slowly into it.

What would have taken twenty minutes if he hadn't cared about noise took an hour when he couldn't make a sound. He'd accomplished it though, and the rickety bed was history. He hadn't ordered a new one.

After the lights went out, he stayed a little longer, picturing her climbing the stairs, fixing her dinner, reading in her new chair. Or would she? Was she angry enough to sit in the old one?

"There you are, you lovesick cowboy." Rance came over to stand beside him. "She'll forgive you, bro."

"I wish I could believe that."

"She will." Rance clapped him on the shoulder. "I did."

"I don't know why you did after the way I've behaved. But I'll take it."

"You'd better. If you start dishing out that crap again, I really will go all Jackie Chan on you."

He laughed. "Since when are you into martial arts?"

"I could be. If necessary. Listen, which one of the Armstrong sisters is more my type — Sara or Lani?"

"Remind me which is which."

"Sara's the redhead and Lani's the brunette."

"Neither. They live in *New Jersey*, lamebrain."

"Yeah, but Dallas got Trent to move out here, so Trent could get one of his sisters to come out. I just need to decide which one I should ask him to focus on."

"I'm sure Trent's gonna love this plan of yours, luring one of his sisters out here for your benefit."

"I won't put it like that. Lani's my age and Sara's two years younger. I'm thinking the younger one. She might like the idea of dating an older man."

"How long have you known these ladies? Two hours?"

"More than that! Almost three. But I'm just getting started. They're staying for a week. That gives me plenty of time to maneuver."

"And the girls are bunking in Trent's guest room, as I recall. He works from home. Chaperone, twenty-four-seven. Good luck maneuvering around that setup."

"Better than if they were with their folks at Angie's house. I'm not sure Harry likes me. I'll take my chances with Trent. He's cool. I found out he has bartending experience. I've talked him into moonlighting at the Buffalo."

"No kidding?"

"He needs to get out of that cabin more. Anyway, we're becoming buddies. He'll trust me with his sisters."

"He's their big brother, dude."

"Hey!" Sky yelled from the doorway. "We're doing toasts. Get in here!"

"On our way," Lucky called back.

Rance laid a hand on his arm. "Promise me you'll talk to her tomorrow."

"I promise. I just hope she's willing to listen."

31

Lucky walked Silver around the yard, keeping him warmed up as Buck and Sky organized the troops for Angie's birthday ride on Wednesday morning. He'd never been happier to be part of a family gathering than he was today.

As he kept Silver moving, he looked for ways he could be of help. This year posed the biggest challenge ever. The entire Armstrong contingent had decided to go.

His mom had worked a miracle and tapped neighbors for extra horses. Gentle horses. Dallas was the only one who knew how to ride. The other five had never been on a horse.

At least Trent had the right clothes. Angie had scrounged boots and hats for the women and Dallas had loaned his best boots to his dad while he wore the scruffy ones. He and Angie had their hands full working with both parents and Trent.

Lucky was on his way over to offer a hand when Andy and his mom beat him to it. Good move on their part. They clearly had a soothing effect on the situation. Almost immediately the frowns turned to laughter.

Meanwhile Rance was in his element, impressing Sara and Lani with his cowboying skills. No way was Lucky horning in on that program.

The more he studied the milling group, the more he saw that it wasn't nearly as chaotic as it seemed at first glance. Even the Armstrongs looked more relaxed now that Andy and his mom were there.

Penny, Beau, Cheyenne and Bret all wore baby backpacks. Molly had tucked little Elvira in a front-facing sling. All the kids were bundled up in snowsuits and apparently awestruck. Not a peep out of any of them.

Sam was the most hyper of the bunch, racing from one group to the next, impatient to get the show on the road.

As always on February fourteenth, the weather was gorgeous. Angie must have an in with Mother Nature. That was the only explanation Lucky had for the almost perfect record of sunny skies on her birthday, Valentine's Day, and now her wedding day.

Just because she was getting married in the afternoon didn't mean she couldn't have her traditional family trail ride in the morning, though. That was his little sis, going for the gusto.

His little sis. What a privilege to call her that. After the family meeting he'd spent hours staring into the dark while endlessly reliving the scene at the ranch house. And Rance's reaction to it.

No telling how much time had passed before he'd finally punched through his confusion.

And there it was — the reason his mother had called a meeting with just the ten of them.

She'd called them the *core group.* The center of their strength and power. She'd hoped he'd see it was available to him. Always had been. Always would be.

The evidence had been right there. When she'd summoned them, when she'd said he needed their support, they'd all dropped what they were doing. Because he was a vital part of that core.

The gut-deep knowledge still choked him up. Probably always would. He got it.

He'd spent Tuesday making amends, starting with his mother. She'd cried. He'd cried, too, to be honest.

After they'd made it through the tears, he'd screwed up his courage and asked about opening a bookshop in Apple Grove. Turned out she hadn't pursued it because he hadn't said anything more and all the work would be on him.

Oksana would get a laugh out of that. Well, she would if she hadn't written him off as a lost cause. His family had welcomed his apology with warm hugs and heartfelt words. But they were his core group. They would never write him off.

He was on shakier ground with Oksana. Or was he? Two days ago she'd been in love with him, maybe even as much as he'd been in love with her.

She'd confessed to having a crush for eighteen months. Her feelings ran deep. She wasn't the type to fall out of love in forty-eight hours.

Chances were good she still loved him. But she probably didn't like him very much. He couldn't blame her. He hadn't been particularly fond of himself, either.

Early this morning, as he'd trimmed his beard, he'd found himself smiling at the guy in the mirror. That guy was part of a core group. No wonder his mother had named him Lucky.

* * *

From his position as the last groomsman in the lineup, Lucky flat-out couldn't see the front door of the church. It was located several feet from the arched entrance to the chapel.

The minister could see it just fine. Dallas and Trent had a great view. So did Sky and Beau. Cheyenne and Clint would have to lean a little, but after that, the rest of them were S.O.L.

Rance gave him a nudge. "Stop fidgeting."

"What if she doesn't come?" He kept his voice low, although the music would likely cover any quiet conversation.

Angie had hired a guitarist and a fiddle player from the band currently playing at the Buffalo. For the intro she'd chosen instrumentals of old favorites from the likes of George Strait and Garth Brooks. Word had it the guitarist would sing during the processional.

"If she doesn't come," Rance said under his breath, "then while we're at the reception, you slip over there and say your piece. Don't worry. It's not like she's leaving town."

"I hadn't even considered that. What if she went to see her folks? What if she drove there after closing the—"

"What if Mom catches you working your jaw when you're supposed to be focused on Angie's wedding?"

He sighed. "You're right." Although she might not notice since she and Andy were over on the bride's side of the church, heads together as if they might be talking, too. They were also holding hands. Maybe this ceremony would inspire them to set a date.

Normally Buck and Marybeth would be sitting next to them, but Angie had asked Buck to walk her down the aisle and Marybeth to be a bridesmaid. Sweetest choices ever.

And strategic. With Kendall as her matron of honor and Marybeth occupying the first bridesmaid slot, Angie could match up the rest of the couples starting with Sky and Penny. Rance would partner with Lani and he'd get Sara.

The Wenches took turns monitoring the guest book and ushering guests into the chapel. Most likely they'd requested the ushering job. The Wagon Train Fire Department was in attendance and those ladies clearly enjoyed showing those burly firefighters to their seats.

As the church filled, Lucky's chest tightened. Where was she? Every damn time he saw movement through that arch, he held his breath.

Was that a flash of red? Probably Colleen. Or not. He gasped as Annette escorted Oksana into the chapel. Annette paused, searching for an empty seat.

Oksana took that moment to look directly at him, head high, gaze triumphant. Tall? She *owned* tall. Those red stilettos and an updo defiantly added inches. God, she was magnificent.

He couldn't control his happy grin as he held her gaze. She'd done it. She'd made a glorious Sigourney Weaver entrance.

And her red dress... wow. While there was no scooped neck to highlight cleavage or slit up the side to give a glimpse of leg, the material clung lovingly to her curves, subtle, yet even more seductive as a result. Dancing with her would be—

Whoa, boy. You have a truck-load of apologizing before you have a prayer of that happening.

Guests in the back pew scooched together to make room for her and she broke eye contact so she could work her way into the empty spot. Thanks to her updo, he could still see the top of her head.

She'd done her part. She'd come to Angie's wedding. The rest was up to him.

32

That sweet grin of delight had turned Oksana to mush. That was the Lucky who'd stolen her heart. Was he back?

Her view was partially blocked by a number of broad-shouldered firefighters in the groom's section of the chapel. She only caught glimpses of him as the guys shifted in their seats.

He looked gorgeous as always. The familiar outfit — a vest, Western cut jacket and dress Wranglers — emphasized every swoon-worthy attribute of that cowboy. Evidently the McLintock brothers had found a look that worked for these occasions and they'd stuck with it.

Their decision to line up in birth order touched her. They'd done the same for Marsh and Ella's wedding in August. Lucky was last, since he'd been born a couple of hours after Rance.

His position was the same as it had been six months ago. So were his clothes. He'd worn a beard then, too. But he looked different.

Before she could figure out why, the music changed and the guitarist began singing an up-tempo rendition of Dustin Lynch's *Cowboys and Angels.*

A cute redhead Oksana hadn't met danced through the arched doorway carrying a red and white bouquet and wearing a dress with a skirt that fluttered around her knees. A brunette in a matching dress came next, sashaying up the aisle in time to the music.

Oksana chuckled. She'd been so focused on Lucky she'd missed the red and white bouquets at the end of the pews, arrangements tied with red and white bows and decorated with glittering hearts. She should have guessed Angie would lean into Valentine's Day.

Faye appeared next and danced down the aisle. Tyra, Molly and Ella followed. Evidently red was the perfect color to wear to this wedding. Angie had chosen it for all her attendants.

Jess and Penny continued the procession, followed by a diminutive woman whose face was alight with joy as she pranced into the chapel, her skirt whirling around her knees. She'd turned her silvery braid into a crown embellished with red rosebuds and tiny hearts.

Oksana did a double-take. Marybeth! She'd never seen her in anything but a shirt and pants, even at Ella's wedding. But she'd put on a red dress and fancied up her hair for this event. As she two-stepped down the aisle, a ripple of applause went through the crowd.

They loved it. So did the McLintocks, who all wore grins a mile wide. Marybeth was a hit.

Kendall, Angie's matron of honor, looked lovely dancing down the aisle, but there was no competing with Marybeth's transformation.

At least, not until the music ended and a hush fell over the chapel. It was Angie's turn.

The musicians launched into Russell Dickerson's *Yours,* and Angie appeared on Buck's arm, the two of them framed in the arched doorway. Rising to their feet, the guests faced the bride.

Oh, yeah, that girl had nailed it. She'd ditched her tomboy self, gone against type, and covered herself in yards of white chiffon and lace. She'd left her dark curly hair down in a beautiful cascade of curls. She was radiant. And Dallas was awestruck. His dazed expression brought a lump to Oksana's throat.

Buck glanced down at Angie and his chest heaved. Murmuring something, Angie gave his arm a squeeze and they started walking slowly down the aisle.

The words of the love song tugged hard at Oksana's heart. She glanced at Lucky. He was looking at her. Oh, God, was he ever looking at her. The man who had walked out on her Monday night was gone. Lucky was back.

* * *

A wedding reception was a lousy place to have an important conversation. Lucky had gone over what he wanted to say a million times but despaired of ever finding a time to say it.

Or a place. On New Year's his mom had taken Andy back to Clint and Tyra's office for a chat, but tonight the kids were bedded down in there.

That left precious little private space in the Buffalo for a talk that could change his life and hers.

He was grateful for the wedding, though, because it had sharpened his focus. Every aspect had resonated — the song lyrics, the words of the ceremony, the love flowing between Angie and Dallas as they promised to cherish that love for a lifetime.

He was grateful for the reception, too because theoretically he'd have a chance to tell Oksana what was in his heart. Theoretically.

Hey, maybe now? During this lull in the toasting? He pushed back his chair, ready to seize the moment and ask her to dance.

Then Angie piped up. "Hey, everybody. Ella's drinking club soda instead of champagne. I didn't notice until just now. Ella and Marsh, is there something you'd like to tell us?"

Everyone's attention shifted. Ella and Marsh exchanged a glance.

"C'mon," Angie said. "You've been made. You probably didn't want to say anything since this is our show, but since I'm the bride, I'm calling you out."

Ella grinned. "Okay, okay, we're pregnant."

A cheer went up from the group. The prospective new grandparents, all four of them, plus Ella's sister Faye, rushed the couple to give them hugs.

"And we're not the only ones," Marsh shouted over the hubbub. "Check that glass Jess is holding!"

"Snitch!" Beau shouted back. "If you just overloaded Mom's circuits, that's on you."

Everyone laughed, but his mom did look like she'd erupt into a Fourth of July fireworks display as she raced over to grab Jess and Beau in a tight hug. Andy was right behind her.

Eventually everyone settled down. Sort of, except for the questions about due dates and who would be first. Turned out the due dates were within days of each other.

Then his mom and Andy put their heads together for a moment. She nodded and he stood. "Dez and I had planned to tell you this later since we didn't want to claim the spotlight, either, but since that program is out the window, we—"

"You've set a date?" Rance leaped to his feet. "Is it May? Please say it's May. That's such a great—"

"It's May, son. May eleventh. We decided it would be appropriate to get married on Mother's Day weekend."

The room went wild, this time converging on Andy and his mom. So did he. When he finally got a chance to hug his mother, she put her mouth close to his ear. "Have you talked with Oksana?"

He drew back. "Not yet. It's so noisy and I—"

She lowered her voice. "Take her back to the bookshop."

"I can't leave the party yet. It's too early."

"I'm not suggesting you *stay* there. Not now, anyway. Go over, straighten things out, and come back. We're all dying for you to fix this."

"Yes, ma'am." He turned around and Oksana was right behind him. Yep, they were eye-to-eye, just like they'd been when she'd worn those shoes Saturday night. "Hey, there."

"Hey, there, yourself." Her gaze was steady. "I came over to say hi and congrats to your mom and Andy. I think it's exciting they've set a date."

"Sure is. Listen, after you talk to her, would you consider walking over to the bookshop with me so we can talk?"

She blinked. "You mean leave the party?"

"Not permanently." He could see the wheels turning. "Look, it's not what you're thinking."

"What do you think I'm thinking?"

"That I have something besides talking in mind."

"Do you?"

"No! I mean, yes, maybe, in the future, depending, but not..." He sucked in a breath. "We'll come back to the party, I promise. I just want to talk."

She looked like she was trying hard not to smile. "Okay. I left my coat on my chair if you'd like to fetch it for me."

"I'll do that." In no time he'd put on his rented jacket, which wasn't warm enough for walking around town at this hour. He'd counted on transporting himself by truck and hadn't bothered with his heavier one.

He took Oksana's red parka from a chair at the table where she'd been sitting with Annette, Colleen and Colleen's husband George.

He took the opportunity to thank Colleen and Annette again for filling in for him at the shop.

"You're welcome." Colleen glanced at Oksana's coat. "Are you two leaving?"

"Just for a bit. We— I had a question about something to do with the shop, and it's noisy here, so we're—"

"Is everything okay at the shop?" Annette frowned. "It all seemed fine when we left yesterday."

"It's just... I need to talk to her privately."

Colleen gazed at him and smiled. "Lucky, you don't have to make up a story. I've known you since you were in diapers. I've seen the way you look at Oksana and the way she looks at you. I hope the *talk* goes well."

"Thank you." Face hot, he swung around and scanned the room, eager to escape. Oksana was heading his way so he walked to meet her and helped her on with her parka. Even that slight contact gave him the shakes. "Let's go."

He motioned her past the wooden buffalo, who moaned *Aaand theyyyy lived haaaapily everrr aaafterrr.* He followed quickly and the sensor didn't have time to reset. Then he opened the door for her.

"You'll be cold if that rented jacket is all you're wearing."

"It'll do. Besides, your feet'll be cold. Want to take my truck?"

She stepped into the cold night air. "Why, so you can show me how clean it is inside?"

He laughed. "The cab's clean but the bed still has slivers of particle board in it."

"I don't want to take your truck. Let's just walk fast."

"In those shoes?"

"I'll be fine. Let's do it." She started across the street and lengthened her stride.

So did he. "You look gorgeous, by the way."

"Thanks. You, too." Her breath fogged the air but she wasn't laboring to breathe.

Impressive conditioning. "I've never seen you wear your hair like that. Looks good."

"I don't do it often. Too much work."

"The ponytail looks nice, too. But the best is when you wear it down, because then I can—" He stopped in the middle of the street. "Oksana, I love you. I love you so much."

She whirled toward him, eyes wide.

"I've been a total jerk. You have every right to put me through the wringer for what I've done, what I've said, and I—"

Hurling herself at him, she almost knocked him down. "What wringer?" She wrapped her arms around his neck. "I don't see any wringers around here. I just see the man I love."

He hugged her close, heart pounding. "You forgive me? Just like that? You forgive me?"

"Of course I do. All I needed was an apology. You can't beat one that starts with *I love you*." She kissed him, her lips cold at first, but they quickly grew warmer. Then hot.

His good sense evaporated in the heat of her kiss, which promised him lovemaking the likes of which he'd never had. Considering what he'd already enjoyed with this woman, that was saying something.

He unzipped her coat and slid his hands around her waist, pulling her in tight against his needy body. He had no plan, just a craving that grew stronger by the second.

Then she eased away from the kiss, but only a little bit. The brisk walk hadn't made her pant, but that kiss had. "I interrupted you, though." She dragged in a breath. "I didn't let you finish your apology. Is there more?"

"Only this. Thanks to my family…" He had to stop for air, too. "I have my head on straight."

"That's good."

"And I hope you'll take me back because…" He gulped. This was the biggie, for all the marbles. "Because then I can ask you to marry me."

Her breath hitched. "I take you back."

"Then will you—"

"Yes." And she started kissing him again.

"Hey, bro!"

Was that Rance? How could that be Rance? Oksana drew back again. "It's Rance."

"What's he doing?"

"Coming out of the Buffalo."

He turned his head, and sure enough, his crazy brother was on his way and he hadn't put on a heavy coat, either.

"Get back in there," he called out. "That jacket won't keep you warm enough."

"I won't be out here long. We've been watching through the window, expecting to see you two go into the bookshop. Instead you've stalled out in the middle of the street. Judging from the steam you're generating, we don't think there's a chance in hell you'll be coming back to the party."

Oksana looked over at him. "Good call."

"Since we all have a stake in the outcome, I volunteered to brave the bitter cold, get the 411 and report back."

Lucky glanced at Oksana. "When he says they all have a stake, he's talking about the core group — me, my siblings and Mom."

Her expression softened. "I see."

"Lucky's got it right about the core group, but I'd say pretty much everyone in the Buffalo is invested at this point. What should I tell them?"

Oksana focused on Lucky, a soft glow in her dark eyes. "Tell them we're very much in love and we're going to get married."

Joy bloomed in his chest. "Yeah, we are." He tucked her in closer.

"Awesome! They'll be overjoyed. Oh, and a word of advice. Take this operation to the bookshop. You're putting on a great show, but I'm worried you'll get frostbite on your privates."

Oksana giggled.

"Goodbye, Rance." Lucky held her gaze and smiled. "Want to move inside where it's warmer?"

"Are you cold?"

"No, ma'am."

"Me, either, but I suppose eventually we'll want to take off our clothes. That could be problematic."

"The town does have ordinances."

"Then just kiss me one more time and we'll go in. Make it a good one. Let's show 'em this is for keeps."

"Damn straight." When he claimed her mouth, heat rushed through his veins, as it always had. But now love poured from his heart, too. Calm, steady and nourishing, it flowed easily, without pain, without doubt.

For the first time in his life, he stood on solid ground.

New York Times bestselling author Vicki Lewis Thompson's love affair with cowboys started with the Lone Ranger, continued through Maverick, and took a turn south of the border with Zorro. She views cowboys as the Western version of knights in shining armor, rugged men who value honor, honesty and hard work. Fortunately for her, she lives in the Arizona desert, where broad-shouldered, lean-hipped cowboys abound. Blessed with such an abundance of inspiration, she only hopes that she can do them justice.

For more information about this prolific author, visit her website and sign up for her newsletter. She loves connecting with readers.

VickiLewisThompson.com

9 781638 039259